Hunters in the Snow

Hunters in the Snow

A Collection of Short Stories by

David Kranes

THE UNIVERSITY OF UTAH PRESS ⌇ 1979

The author wishes gratefully to acknowledge permission from the following
to include previously published stories:

"Diving Lesson," copyright 1970, and "Little Sister," copyright 1974, reprinted by permission from *The Western Humanities Review*.

"The Wishbone," copyright 1965, reprinted by permission from the *Trans-
atlantic Review*.

"The Frame Lover," copyright 1972, and "Peterson's Stones," copyright
1976, reprinted by permission from the *Michigan Quarterly Review*.

"Hunt," copyright 1976 by the University of Northern Iowa, reprinted by
permission from *The North American Review*.

"Dealer," copyright 1973, reprinted by permission from *Esquire*.

"Cordials," copyright 1975, reprinted by permission from *Tri-quarterly*.

For my parents

Contents

Diving Lesson

They did things together. Not all the time, not in any organized or practice-session way, but the boy and his father were found together frequently. It might be on a lawn, sitting, or in a drugstore, buying film (which usually led to a Milky Way or a root beer). Most often it was in the car, connecting points with home, sketching a huge misshapen asterisk on an Esso map, centering it just north of Boston.

The boy was eleven. The father, thirty-seven. They looked somewhat alike. Men in gas stations, girls at Howard Johnson counters said so anyway. They both liked mocha chip ice cream; they both liked dragonflies. And although they could not agree on Plymouths or chicken livers, they did things together and were close. They knew about each other, and each, because it was a strangely warming thought, liked to think there was a mystery in the knowledge.

One late afternoon in July, an afternoon which was clear and smelled of warm rocks and tar and baking leaves and water evaporating from plastic wading pools, the father came home early from his work. The mother was out. He left her a note.

"How'd you like to go up swimming, up to Marblehead for an hour or so? Cool off."

"O.K.," the boy said.

"Just O.K.?"

"No," the boy said, "no, *more* . . . good!"

"O.K.," the father said. They smiled.

The boy did not ask about his mother. It was not her but their world, his and his father's. The baby girl and the mother had theirs. It had its own privacy. And mysteries would grow up there, too, the boy assumed, women's mysteries that he would leave uninvaded . . . or try.

Both changed to bathing suits, took towels, and brought underwear and fresh pants to change to after the swim. It was the only time that clothes smelled really clean, when you slipped into them after swimming, when they had lain where the sun could reach them in your car, on the back window ledge, and were warm and weighed nothing. The father patted his boy below one shoulder, and they entered the car.

Driving was driving; they talked.

"What happened to the Sox today?" the father asked.

"Crumby!" the boy answered. "Four errors in the eighth. Seven to three!"

"Wait."

"For what?"

"August's their month," the father said and smiled.

"April's their month," the boy said; "spring training."

They laughed.

"See that?" the father pointed. The boy saw houses everywhere, pastel houses with crooked, angular roofs, saw shrubless lawns and cedar carports and the toy skywriting of tiny lawn sprinklers. "Used to be all one farm," the father went on. "Worked there one summer when I was . . . younger once. Cavenaugh. They were the family that owned it. Nice farm."

"Looks just like Natick," the boy said.

"Yes," the father said, and he brought his jaw forward to a set.

And so it went — driving, talking. Lawns yellowed to marsh grass, then to marsh meadows interrupting block neighborhoods, finally to lone houses, older and more positioned, tougher and more secure. The wind brined. The road, it seemed, thinned steadily; or perhaps it was just the close marshes insisting more on the road.

At last their car pulled up to a small beach on an inlet of the Atlantic. Sometimes they went to large beaches where there were breakers. Sometimes they came here. Here it was quiet. There was a small floating raft they could swim to, sit and feel strong and tired on together. Gulls relaxed here. Thirty transistor radios didn't dispute. Here they felt balanced: just themselves, some water, and some sky.

It was near suppertime. Signs, "No Fires," sent people with briquet gear elsewhere. This was a swimming beach. You could not shut your eyes, breathe, and think you might be in Howard Johnson's parking lot. Only one other family neighbored them, a group of five, and this, way down the beach, rose now, one by one, brushing off sand. They looked hungry; even at fifty yards, hungry and burned. The father and the boy left the car, stood together.

Tufts and raw clumps of grass bunched a coarse border between the parking lot and beach. The two started across them, their walking unbalanced, the grass, crisp. Just where the grass gave way to sand the father saw an amethystine gleam. He bent and picked something up. The boy watched. It was a large jagged section of a Coke bottle.

"So many weapons these days," the father said—then frowned. He held the glass fierce and sleeping in his open hand as if it were an infant sparrow with a broken wing. The distant family, standing and milling now, shook out rough flurries of sand from its beach blankets.

"Should we find all the pieces?" the boy asked.

The father looked over. "Good idea," he said finally, and they knelt, sorting the sand to find the missing bottle in blades. They did it quickly, dropping the pieces carefully into a nearby rusting barrel, then moving off again toward softer sand.

"How about right here?" the father asked, kicking off his moccasins, nodding down to the boy.

"Sure," the boy said. "Great. There's no one."

"Can you still make it to the raft?" the father asked. They could hear the slight churning of the surf from where they stood.

"If you go down, I'll save you," the boy said, drawing his T-shirt quickly over his head.

The father unbuttoned his shirt. The two of them walked quietly to the water's edge. They stood there together looking out, letting the dry salt wind, the heat of it, hold them, free their minds.

They stood in the same sure oblivion men stand in sometimes under a shower, warm, relaxed. Gulls and ospreys gathered the air above them, but went unseen.

"Nice," the father said.

"Nice," the son followed.

"Glad we decided to do it."

"Me too."

Then the father broke their station, wandering slowly out through the slight ruffles of water. The son followed. The son yelled "Hey!" and crashed the water with his body beside the father, began swimming. Some of the splashed water struck the father's pale chest and felt cold, but the father watched his boy cut the water toward the raft, cut it smoothly, swimming as he had taught him to swim or at least a refinement of those lessons. The father smiled. The son swam well. The water curled now over the father's bathing suit, struck his navel nearly electrically. Still, he smiled.

Then, abruptly, there were two bodies exciting the water, the larger one closing the gap on the one that was smaller. The father and the son swam hard at the same raft, each aware of the other, each pretending that it was of course not a contest, but each prideful that it was. A foam; a wake; a short flurry of blurred water: they drove ahead. Both felt their hearts and muscles stretched. Both felt excited. The son touched the raft a clear second before his father but knew the ritual well enough to say nothing of it. They both pulled themselves up. Neither used the ladder.

When he had caught his breath, the father said, "You've been practicing."

"Nope," the son said. "Not really."

"You *must* have been practicing. I can't be getting *that* old."

"You had twice the distance."

"I guess that's right."

Give and take, a fine game. They left it there, stood up, looked back to the gray-yellow band of beach, measuring their feat.

"Fifty yards?" the father asked.

"I thought it was about a hundred," the boy said honestly, still breathing hard.

"That's a hell of a short football field," the father said, gauging it with a smile and a squint. The boy said nothing. He was embarrassed. "That's a good sixty, though," the father added. "At least sixty. Pretty good."

The family there before them now piled into its car. The swimmers watched. From their raft they saw three rear ends disappear into a back seat, saw the man lift the trunk of his car, saw him close it, saw him open it, take out a package of something and close it again, saw him eat something from the package, open the trunk, put the package back, start to close the trunk, pause, then slam it down. They watched the man wipe his mouth. They watched him climb into the car, shut the door, open the door, walk around to the back of the car, open the trunk, take out what looked like the same package, move to the front of the car, thrust it through the open window, open the front door, climb in, slam the door, get out, slam the trunk, and return. Then the car started, blue mist ballooning from its exhaust pipe, and pulled away. It shrank quickly. It flattened, became almost transparent, interfering with neither marsh nor sky as it disappeared down the track of road.

"What do you think?" the father asked. "MacDonald's or Carvell's?"

"Carvell's." The boy hardly considered it.

The father nodded. "I think you're right." He nodded more. "I think you're right on the button that time."

"Ate half the cookies himself, then put them in the trunk." The boy laughed. The father laughed, laughed in spite of himself. "Boy, you'd never do something like that. Put cookies in the trunk. Bet they were marshmallow, too. Big fat marshmallow cookies. You know, with that fuzz, that coconut fuzz stuff on them. The pink and white ones. Boy, you'd never . . ."

"Who knows?" The father stared at the car's vanishing point. ". . . Who can tell?"

"What do you mean?" the boy asked.

"Hmmm?" the father toned, still looking away.

"What do you mean, 'who can tell?' You said, 'who can tell?' " the boy asked him.

"Oh . . ." The father slapped his own stomach, rubbed it in place a bit. "Oh, I don't know. Just thinking out loud, I guess." He pushed narrowly at a smile.

The boy watched him. He watched the tightness of his face: his pressed lips, narrow eyes, his mind. He watched the father and was not sure what he should say next. "*You* never put cookies in the trunk," he tried.

"You never *looked* there — did you?" The father smiled again. "I've got my life savings there — stashed away. My wrench. My jack. My spare tire." He laughed to himself. "How would you like a diving lesson?" he asked the boy.

"I know how to dive," the boy said.

"Deep?"

"Well . . ." the boy hesitated, "pretty deep."

"I'll show you how to dive *really* deep," the father told him, "so deep that when you cut the water there's hardly a ripple. That's the way the professionals do it. You just sort of disappear into the water and nobody really knows where you've gone or whether, yes, or whether anybody's even *dived* there. It's all technique."

"O.K.," the boy said.

"Then, when you come up, it's a surprise." The father laughed. "Nobody's expected it, and . . . there you are!"

"Good!" The boy was smiling now. "How do you do it?"

"Well," the father said, "first . . . " And he explained the principles: height, then feet toward the sky, toes pointed, knees straight, hands open and straight ahead to break the fall if need be, eyes open to see the bottom, to know where it is. "Resiliency," the father concluded, "spring! If you can get it. Now there's no board here, so I'll have to get as much as I can from my own legs. Which is not necessarily a bad thing," he said privately.

The boy listened. The water, air, raft, sand, approach of

evening, all composed. Terns wrote the father's sentences in easy flight. The ribbon road, meandering as it was, came *to* this place, did not unravel *from* it. The father placed his toes at the raft's edge. "Like this," he said.

He sprang. Motion returned — up. Then he reversed himself. Toes, fingertips changed in swift motion, and the father was heading down again. The frame, straight and practiced, cut water with no splash. The body followed. Toes vanished a foot, less than a foot, from the raft. There was a turbulence, a slight white foam, an agitation perhaps; not rightly a splash. A casual bather, sunning on the beach, would have seen nothing. A watchful bather might have sensed, if anything, a rhythm but would never have connected that rhythm with the father's wet, moment-later surfacing. "Something like that," the father said, pulling himself up on the raft again. "Try it."

"That was great," the boy said.

"Try it," the father said again, standing sleek and glistening, casting a narrow, almost skeletal shadow across the raft planks into the water.

The boy moved slowly to the edge until his toes overhung the wood. His chest swelled with breathing. He considered the mechanism of himself, his body, the air, the water, his father's example. "How did you get so high?" he finally asked.

"Spring from the balls of your feet; use your knees. Bring your arms around and then straight up — break the clouds with them." The father mimed it, then slapped his stomach.

The boy mimed it once and then stood thinking. The father watched. There was no comment in his watching. It was regard, pure and uncomplicated. Suddenly the boy lifted from the raft — up. He rose as the father had: with less grace, to less height, with no confidence, but rose. Then, at the peak, he faltered. His body convulsed, lay horizontal for a pale second, convulsed less awkwardly, then managed to enter the water head first. There was a large curling splash. A white lip of water separated and extended visibly for some distance. The father watched the water settle, watched the surface unlather, studying it. The boy surfaced some distance away.

"Jeez!" the boy said.

"That was all right," the father told him.

The boy swam hard back to the raft. He pulled himself up. "Boy, was that lousy!" he said not really to himself but more in the hope that the father might contradict. The father understood.

"You started fine," he encouraged. "Moved up. Good spring. When you feel you're nearing the top of it, though," and he mimed the reversal, the head's ultimate alignment with gravity, "try to feel the height. Try to get a sense of the top of it. So that you know when you're there. So that it doesn't bother you. So that you don't find yourself going down when you think you're still going up. Watch again," the father said.

Once again the father demonstrated. There was less wonder in it now, more fact to be observed and understood. Rise, turn, dive, slice the water, submerge — the boy studied the steps carefully. He nodded to himself without knowing it. The whole process made more sense to him now. The father returned. The boy readied himself.

This time the dive was smoother, first to last. There were rough moments in the flow, but the dive was smoother. "Felt better," the boy said, rising from the water nearer the raft.

"Looked better." The father smiled.

The boy smiled to himself and churned back to the raft. "How were my legs that time?" the boy asked, climbing up.

"A bit apart," the father said. "Try for more arch this time, too, coming down."

"Do it." He sought a model.

The father dove. The boy dove.

"That's it!" the father called as the boy shot, smiling, to the surface.

The boy returned and dove again.

"You've got it!" The father congratulated him.

The boy swam slowly, gracefully back to the raft, boosted himself in a strong, lazy motion onto the planks. "Thanks," he said, tossing the water from his wet hair. "It's not so bad if you work on it."

"No, it's not. It's not bad if you work on it. That's right." The father struck him gently on the back. The two stood quietly. They looked out toward the bay's mouth, their backs to shore. The air was still warm and the smell of salt grew with the widening sun which sank now, it seemed, almost vertically. "See that?" the father asked. He pointed out to a small dust speck on the horizon.

"Smoke?"

"Very good." The father judged him. "Probably a steamer. Maybe a cruise — Boston to Nova Scotia."

They stood in silence a while longer, drying, feeling their skins tighten with it, the pores seal.

"How come you got out early today?" the boy asked, looking up.

"Mr. Prentiss said it was too hot to see it through till five. I agreed with him."

There was a pause. Some tiny gnats penciled the air around them. The boy picked it up again.

"You used to boss Mr. Prentiss, didn't you?" he asked.

"Yes," said the father. "You could put it that way."

"And now he does you?"

"Does . . . ?"

"Bosses, I mean."

"Oh . . . yes. Yes."

"You used to boss Mr. Prentiss; and now he bosses you." The boy put two halves of a simple history together, then paused. "Why is that?"

"Ohhh . . ." The father cocked his elbow, his arm even with the ground, and stared at the white untanned band and circle on his arm where his watch had been.

"Why's that? I mean I like you better than Mr. Prentiss. I'd think most people would."

"Well, I like *you* better than Mr. Prentiss. But that doesn't mean you should be his boss." The father smiled.

"But if you used to be his boss, why didn't you *stay* being his boss? That's what I mean."

The two were looking at each other.

"Well, maybe . . ." The father puffed his cheeks slightly. "Maybe Mr. Prentiss *bosses* better than I do. Does that — does that make any sense at all?"

The boy thought. He started to nod a little bit to himself. Then he stopped. Finally he nodded again, stronger but still tentatively. The father wet his lips, took a breath, pressed his lips together, opened his mouth to speak.

"But you weren't *fired* or anything?" The boy asked, looking up again. The father saw his son and loved him. He marvelled at the height and depth of the human heart: magic; magic dimensions. "Dad . . . ?"

The father smiled. "No," he said; "no, I wasn't fired." He moved to the edge of the raft. ". . . Or anything."

He bent his legs, threw up his arms, and sprang up admirably into the air. The raft jarred. The son watched. The sun, air, sea, even time of day were so quiet they seemed to catch the father at the top of his dive and hold him there an instant in still life. Released, he fell, slicing the water only an inch from the raft — a fine dive.

The boy watched the water. He watched it swirl and circle where his father's toes had disappeared. He thought about their talk, his questions and his father's answers. He hadn't quite understood really why he had asked the questions that he had.

Small bubbles surfaced just beneath him and broke. The boy felt strange. He was struck suddenly with a terror. Where *was* his father? His body had fallen so fast, so straight, so near the spot that it had lifted from: what if it kept on falling? What if his father fell straight down through the water into the mud, into the ooze, through it, beneath it? What if his toes disappeared *there* just as they had beneath the flaking bay water because he was unable to break his fall? The boy's chest tightened.

"Dad . . . ?" he called tentatively.

More bubbles rose to the surface and broke.

"Dad?" He started almost to cry. The beach was bare. Stiff, gliding gulls, like dumb, laundered shrouds, sailed over his head. He poised and, without even a small child's prayer, dove. He did not know that his father had angled and set out under water to test his wind. The father rose. They missed each other. The father, assuming that the boy was still on the raft, started a slow stroking back to it.

The boy sank, fought his way down. He searched the bottom for some hand or foot, some flesh to take hold of and rescue. His mind screamed the father's name, pleaded it. And even under water he cried so that the whole sea, except its coldness, seemed his doing. He swallowed some water, choked on it, twisted his body to resolve the pain. The father swam nearly directly above him now.

The boy took in some water and became dizzy. "Dad!" his mind cried; "Daddy, *please!*" He was at the mud now, confused, clawing it. His father's hands cut water. His own small hands cut slime, tore it away. His mind tricked him, inverted the universe. Somehow he saw the mud above him and felt he had to get through it to live. He tore wretchedly, dizzily, digging. It came away in clutches, fistfuls of mud, fouling the water around him. He was wild. He choked.

Dirt filtered up. It rose. The father, swimming, saw the water around him suddenly color, checked his boy's absence, drew all possible air from the sky, and submerged.

He saw clouds, brackish, slow-rising clouds of ocean scum, then saw his son. He swam down, struggled down toward him, grabbed his hand, tried to pull him up.

But the boy had lost sense. Someone was forcing him down, he thought, and he kicked fiercely at the father. They fought, both for the same life. The boy lashed. The father's face bled from his son's fingernails. His chest ached from a kick. The struggle slacked. The boy went limp. And with one thud of the father's feet against the mud bottom, they were moving up.

They broke the surface. The father's lungs devoured air. The boy's did not. The father pushed at the boy's stomach and forced some water out. He cried, but swam, holding his boy's limp, tired head above water. Blood poured into the father's heartbeat. He could not tell whether the son's own heart beat or merely echoed.

They reached the raft. The father pushed the boy up onto the planks until he hung hemplike over the edge. He started to climb up. But as he rose, he suddenly sensed the limp body above him slipping back down and away. He grabbed instinctively, caught the wrist, and managed to pull both himself and the boy up onto the wood. The boy still seemed not to be breathing. Blood poured into the father's heartbeat, but it was impossible . . .

Under the father's grip, the boy's midsection rose and fell on the small boards. More water drained. A rhythm began or became noticeable. Then there was breath. It increased, became surer. The father wept, straddling his boy. The boy tried to move. The father rolled him over, kept the rhythm up a moment till the boy's eyes opened.

"You didn't . . ." His voice was drowsy.

"*Easy!*" The word sounded harsh. The father's forehead was unnaturally dry. He spoke sparely, going far beneath his emotions for control. "Take it easy, son. Focus down." He moved off, keeping one hand on the boy, guiding small breaths. "Took in . . . took in a little water." The father struggled for a voice, one without panic, for his son. "You'll be O.K."

The boy squinted. It seemed amazing really that his muscles were so quickly repaired, even the slight ones. "You dove," the boy asked finally.

"I . . ." In his mind, the raft inverted, forsook sky like a plastic and capsized tub-toy, then righted itself. Pieces of broken coke bottle, rubbish, pressed on the father's lungs. "I dove; and then you dove — yes. And we . . . both came up." The father fumbling somehow for his own name, clutched at the moment when he and the mother, both of them sitting in the unsleepable dark of their bedroom late in an eighth month, had named the boy. "Keep quiet for a minute more," he said almost sternly. "Just breathe." He took his hand off and let the parts work by themselves. The boy's eyes opened wider. He watched above. The man watched him. Dragonflies, trying to thread the raft, watched the man.

"Look at that, Dad," he said finally. "The gulls — must be coming down for fish."

"There's an instinct," the father said, "keeps us from crashing. They . . . make it work for them. Don't they?"

"Yeah. Gee — look at that!"

They sat and talked for a half-hour, maybe more. The boy sat up after a while, then stood, walking around the raft, pointing things out to his father who commented only slightly or asked a question. The sky was well shadowed now, a few clouds with neon edges but no sun visible. A chalked half-moon managed its plot of sky with some command. The air was cooler. What muscles the water and wind might be said to have seemed relaxed.

"Well, what do you say?" The father spoke, appraising the boy, "Since we left the sleeping bags at home, I guess we'd better not plan to spend the night." And then he smiled.

"No, I guess not." The boy returned it.

"Try it again," the father instructed. "Only . . . level out a little sooner."

"Yeah — I guess," the boy said and stepped toward the beach side of the raft.

The father fingered a whitewashed splinter still lodged in his left palm. "You've got it down pretty well," he said. "I don't need to say anything."

The boy stood there, toes overlapping. "Little nervous after the last time." He smiled tensely.

"Sure. Who wouldn't be. Who wouldn't be." The man observed.

"Yeah, guess so," the boy said. "Well . . ."

"Well . . ."

The boy brought his arms around, lifted nicely into the air, rose, reversed himself straight and pretty and cut the water. The father held his breath. The boy surfaced. They breathed together.

"Nice one!" the father said. "Beauty, in fact."

"Thanks."

"Go ahead. Slow and easy. I'll be with you in a minute. No race this time." He paused. "After all, how much beating can a man *take* in one day?"

"O.K." And the boy set out, swimming as the father had told him, slow and easy. And the father watched. And he thought about how complicated pride was, how simple and how complicated.

The boy had set feet down and was walking now, still in the water. He turned and looked out. "O.K.," he called, not understanding really what it was that he announced.

"Right with you," the father called, and he moved to the edge and dove.

He surfaced. The boy had held his breath. Again father and son breathed together, and the father set out easily toward the shore. The boy stood, stood still and watched. He watched his father swimming toward him. He hoped that, after they changed, they would not go right home but would go out to supper together. He liked being seen in public with the man.

The Wishbone

In October, when I was sixteen, I fell in love with Jane Dennis. Jane lived on Central Park West, and on Saturday nights after I finished my stockboy work at Klein's I'd meet her by the horsecarts on Fifty-ninth Street and we'd do something. Once we saw three movies. Sometimes we'd walk. Jane said we were in "like," but I knew it was deeper than that.

One Sunday, on about our third weekend, we took a bus out to International Airport. It was because we couldn't stay apart. I remember we kissed at four twenty-one on the observation deck. There were jet trails going peach in the sky above us, and we danced (very quietly) to the music they were playing in the United terminal. We held hands on the escalator. We even had mocha sodas and raisin cake in the Savarin Shop. It was raining, and we took another bus back to Manhattan.

At Seventh Avenue, on the corner of Thirty-fourth Street, before we left each other, we kissed again. Maybe it was the soft rain or the lights in Macy's across the street, but I couldn't keep it inside any more.

"Janie?"

"Arnold, I can still hear the planes. Listen!"

"Janie, let's not do it *this* way."

"*Listen* — they're still there. In the sky. Hundreds of jet planes!"

"Let's be . . ." I touched her cheek as softly as I could. It was still raining, but there was only a mist. "Older."

"Arnie?"

"Really older."

Jane lifted her face up against the mist. There was a wind too, small, but Octobery and cold. Jane's blond hair just spilled across her face, and for a minute it was like some movie we'd seen. Then she brushed the hair away and smiled, looking across the street and then up.

"A trillion miles, Arnold, above Macy's," she said; "a trillion, billion miles above their 102d Birthday Sale, there are stars."

"Janie?"

"And there's a very big moon."

She tucked her head between my neck and shoulder, and made small, going-to-sleep sounds.

"Please tell me," I said. And though I hadn't been holding my breath, that was the way it felt.

Jane whispered, "I think it's so beautiful." Then she kissed my ear. I felt sorry for her because I knew my car was cold. But she just turned and ran down into the subway.

I watched her. And when she was gone, I tried to keep some memory picture. It was hard. The only things that came or stayed were her camel's hair coat, the sound of mocha soda going through her straw, and that hair, that beautiful blond hair.

On the next Tuesday, I called her, and we decided some things — about being adults. Jane got an allowance, and I worked. We agreed to save our money. There was this hotel — a friend of my brother's had told me about it — it was in the East Fifties, and you could go there for fifteen dollars without anybody saying anything. And it was *nice*. There was maroon carpeting everywhere, and my brother's friend said there were eleven chandeliers in the lobby.

We picked the day after Thanksgiving, the Friday. That was going to be especially ours. The days weren't very fast at all in getting there, and on the Sunday before, we went out, once again, to the airport. It was November and a really cold day and the whole long bend of terminals seemed brittle, as if they'd break or shatter or something right then.

Things weren't right. Jane didn't say much at all. She just asked me please to stand at the opposite end of the observation deck. So I did. And we stood there looking out into different skies, hearing the roar of different planes. And it all ended with us taking different buses back to the city.

I guessed it was over, that the plans for Friday were off. I didn't even try to call her during the week. Then, on Thanksgiving day, my father called me away from the table to answer the telephone. I had the feeling, when I said hello, that it was the floor manager at Klein's wanting me to work an extra day.

". . . I had a whole drumstick from a twenty-five-pound turkey," she said; "and three helpings of wild rice dressing. Mummy burnt the gravy, but it wasn't too bad."

Something like a bird flew against the inside of my chest. The whole wall that I was looking at turned red for a minute.

"Arnie?"

There was a lot of phlegm in my throat, but I spoke through it. "I had half the skin. My mother made turnip. It really smells terrible, but I had some anyway."

"What about the wishbone?"

"My little sister's drying it with her hair dryer. It's hers!"

"I got ours," she said.

"Did you break it yet?"

"No. Should I bring it tomorrow?"

"Tomorrow?"

"Arnie?"

"Why don't we . . . Bring it tomorrow. Yeah," I said. "Bring it tomorrow. That's a good idea."

"Still two o'clock?" she said.

"Janie?"

"In front of the Public Library?"

My voice was very hoarse. "Two o'clock in front of the Public Library. Bring your wishbone."

"Bye," she said. It was soft.

"Bye."

I hung up, and the house was very quiet. My father belched, and when the rest of the family started talking again, I went to my room, put on my infielder's mitt and cried into the webbing.

I was wearing an olive suit. It was flannel and had a vest, and when I came up from the B.M.T. at Forty-second Street, I could see Jane's camel's hair coat, Jane inside it, standing on the wide Public Library steps.

She had a blue and white knitted scarf thrown back over one shoulder, covering some of her hair. It was like a prep-school or college-weekend scarf, and it didn't help the way I felt. When she saw me coming, she just smiled, did something to straighten the scarf, and let me climb the stairs to where she stood.

"Hi."

"Hi."

"Did you think I wouldn't be here?" she said.

"No. I knew you would if you said you would."

"Did you really?"

"Sure." I said. "Of course."

We looked at each other. It was really quite warm for the day after Thanksgiving.

"Did you bring the wishbone?"

She reached into the pocket of her coat. "See."

It was big, the biggest wishbone I'd ever seen. It could have brought world peace, I bet, or even the Dodgers back to Brooklyn.

"Should we break it now?" She was watching the lights change: green, yellow, red.

"Let's wait."

"O.K." Watching the cars now, she put the bone back and brought out three five-dollar bills. "Here," she said.

"Thanks." And I put them with my own. It made about forty dollars in all.

"Well, let's go." Her hand took mine. "It's almost two-thirty already." She was wearing mittens.

"Isn't it sort of warm for those?" I asked.

"I thought it would be like yesterday — with wind and every-thing," she said.

"Then why don't you take them off?"

"That's all right." And she started down the stairs, bringing me with her.

We walked uptown along Fifth Avenue, talking about things that were in windows.

"That's a nice coffee table," I said.

"Would you ever wear a hat like that?" she asked me.

When we got to Brentano's, Jane stopped and we spent a long time just looking at their display. Finally, when we moved on, Jane said, "What have you heard about *The Making of the President 1960?*" She used the whole title. It was a book with a blue cover.

"Have I told you about Mr. Langler?"

"No. Who's he?"

"My history teacher. He said it was cool."

"*The Making of the President 1960?*"

"Yeah."

"That it was *cool?*"

I nodded. And I wondered who had given her the scarf. "Do you want to watch the skaters for a while?"

"Oh, Arnold!" That's all she said. And we walked by Rockefeller Plaza as if it weren't even there.

When we got to Fifty-eighth Street, we crossed Fifth Avenue and headed east to Second. I stopped at a liquor store to get something for us to drink. Jane insisted that she come in with me. The liquor man was fat, puffy, especially his cheeks, and I wondered if maybe he didn't have any eyes. There was only a pencil line of hair that grew out of a crack in the middle of his head.

"I'd like some Smirnoff Vodka, please." I remembered the ads about the breath.

He looked at us until I could see that he *did* have eyes, very small yellow ones. "One fifth or two?" he said.

"One, I guess."

"You sure?"

"Should I get two?" I asked him.

"Two it is." He took two bottles from the shelf and began to wrap them in green paper. Jane and I stood very still. "That's twelve-forty-eight," he said.

"*How* much?"

"Five-forty-nine apiece plus tax! Twelve-forty-eight." Suddenly it was cold. I felt very cold, but I paid him, and we walked quietly out of the store.

"Does your family have cocktails every night?" Jane asked.

"Just about," I said. But I lied. My parents believed their children shouldn't see them drink. Sometimes late at night, though, I'd hear them getting home.

"Mummy and Daddy do. Sometimes I have sherry." We crossed Lexington Avenue with the light. "I had some sherry yesterday — with the drumstick and the wild rice dressing." She pressed my hand. "But I've never had vodka." I could smell her damp mittens, like a day-camp blanket I'd had once.

"It's good," I said. "Vodka's very good. Especially Smirnoff."

"I've heard." Jane was nibbling some lipstick from the right corner of her mouth.

We crossed Third Avenue. A drop of sweat, smelling very much like a drop of sweat, rolled onto my lips just under my nose. I wondered, if it were colder, whether it would freeze there.

Halfway down the next block was a little boy trying to work a gyroscope on the sidewalk. I loved gyroscopes. I had four of them at home, and I wanted to stop and show him how to pull the string. Jane was walking very close beside me now. She'd hooked her arm in the crook of my elbow, and when we got to the place where the little boy was, together, we walked right by without saying anything. It was the cruelest thing I'd ever done.

From the corner of Fifty-eighth Street and Second Avenue, we could see the hotel, the Regal. Jane smiled and I shifted the bottles so they didn't seem so awkward.

"It looks nice," she said.

It really didn't look *anything* from where we stood. "There's supposed to be maroon carpeting everywhere." I'd mentioned the fact before, but somehow it needed to be said again. "And eleven chandeliers."

"We have a sort of aqua carpeting in our apartment," Jane said. We were still standing at the corner. "Except in the kitchen and bathrooms."

"I like to walk barefoot on rugs," I said.

"You mean when you were *small?*"

"I mean . . ." But I didn't finish. "C'mon."

"Wait a minute," she said. Then she took off her mittens and slipped one hand into mine.

All the way from the corner, I prayed that there wouldn't be a doorman. When we got there, my prayers were answered, and I was disappointed. And the door didn't revolve; it pushed. We went inside, into the lobby, and there was maroon carpeting — *everywhere* — very bright maroon. I counted them, and there were only six chandeliers.

We stood quietly. Once, when I was a lot smaller, I'd been in a big church on a Tuesday, and I'd felt the same way. I kept waiting for something like organ music to begin.

Finally Jane said, "It's nice." And I walked across the carpeting to where a man in a very blue suit stood behind a counter.

"Yes, *sir*," he said.

I told him I'd like a room please.

"Is that for the week, sir?"

"Just today."

"To*day!*"

"I mean until tomorrow," I said.

"But, *sir*, this *is* Thanksgiving weekend."

"You mean you don't have any more rooms?"

"Well, we *do* have *one*. But I'm afraid it's twenty-five dollars. It's our best. It's the bridal suite."

Older, I thought. *That's the whole idea.* "That's all right," I told him. "I'll take it."

"Yes, *sir!*"

I paid. It left me with only two and a half dollars. He gave me a card, and I signed it Mr. and Mrs. Alexander Pitoffsky." Pitoffsky was a kid in school I hated.

"Yes, *sir*," he said again, slapping a little button which rang a bell. A very thin guy with long hair and practically no hips came up. He was wearing a uniform that was an even more awful blue than the manager's. "Paul," the manager said, "show Mr. and Mrs. Pitoffsky to eight-oh-one — would you please?" The scrawny guy took the key.

"Luggage?" he said to me in a sort of a high voice.

I shook my head.

Jane had been sitting in a chair reading *Vogue*. I went over and got her, and before we went upstairs, I bought a copy of the *New York Times*. While we were riding up in the elevator, the scrawny guy stood very stiff and didn't say anything. When the elevator door opened, we followed him down the hall. There was still maroon carpeting — everywhere.

The guy opened the door to 801. Jane walked in. But before I could follow he grabbed my arm.

"You kids shouldn't be doing this," he said.

"What do you mean?"

"You could get in a lot of trouble."

"We're married." I wanted to kick him.

He smiled. "What've you got in the package?"

"Vodka." I tried to say it as though I'd said it a thousand times. "Two fifths," I added, "Smirnoff!"

"You give me one, and nobody will bother you." He smiled again. "I promise, baby." There was something very funny about his jaw.

"Arnold?" Janie was calling from inside.

"Just a minute!" I unwrapped the package and handed him one of the bottles. He looked at it.

"This is only a pint," he said.

I was confused. "It's . . ."

"Only a *pint*, baby," he repeated.

"It's half of all I've got," I said.

He took it. "Thanks, baby," he said. Then he pinched my cheek. "Too bad you're straight." He turned quickly and walked away. I kept wishing that his terrible blue pants would slide down past where his hips should be and send him flying onto the maroon carpeting. But he just stepped into the elevator, not even looking back, and disappeared.

Inside, I locked the door. Jane was sprawled on the edge of the bed, shoes off, camel's hair coat and scarf thrown over a chair. She was watching some football game on television. She looked either eight or twenty-five, and I stood looking at her, trying to decide which. When she saw me, saw that we were alone, she jumped up and ran over to me.

"Oh, Arnie!" she said.

"What's 'straight,' Janie?"

"Straight?"

"Yeah, straight."

"You mean like a line?"

"I don't know. I guess so." Somehow I knew that I really should have kicked him.

She took both my hands, looking at me.

"Who's winning?" I said.

"Nevermind," Jane said — almost as breathlessly as if she'd run two blocks to where I was. Then she kissed me, and her lips were very loose. "This *is* nice, Arnie." She was whispering now. "We are . . . what we wanted to be."

"You mean older?"

"Yes, older." Then she kissed me again. It was hard, almost angry, and it hurt my gums. She started tasting inside my mouth with her tongue, and I was afraid she'd find blood. I kept thinking how glad I was I'd brushed my teeth at noontime, just before I'd left.

It stopped. Then she put her head on my shoulder, and she whispered, "We are, we are!" in my ear very quietly, almost blowing it in. I noticed over her shoulder that her right foot was off the ground, that she was sort of stretching her toes. It was like movie stars do — like a cramp or maybe bathroom pains — something I could never figure out. Then she said, "I'll get the glasses," and ran into the bathroom.

We mixed the vodka with cold water from the tap. Janie sat

where she'd been before on the bed, and I sat in a chair opposite
her. We started talking about kids we both knew, then decided that
it was wrong. It wasn't, it just wasn't the thing to do.

There'd been an election about a month before, and so we
talked about that, who'd won, what it would be like for the next
four years, all the things we'd heard at the supper table at home.
It turned out we'd heard different things. Jane got mad. I tried
not to get mad (the way my father does). We ended up deciding
to consult the *New York Times*. So I read her the editorials.

We had both wanted very much to be drunk, not *sloppy* like
some of the college guys you see in Times Square on Saturday
nights but *sophisticatedly* drunk. But we'd forgotten about it
because the vodka tasted so much like the water. By the time we
got to the editorials, we were on our second glass of whatever it was,
and I had a lot of trouble with some of the words. Second syllables
were impossible — like "unappeasable" was always "un-peasable"
no matter how many times I tried it. Same for "disassociate." We
started laughing. Jane tried to say the words and *she* couldn't.

"Dissssociate!"

"Say the first one, say the 'dis,' then wait a while and say the
rest."

"Dis-"

After about a minute, I said, "O.K."

"Ssssociate!"

We laughed and mixed another glass apiece.

Jane insisted that I read her the book review. It was by somebody with the first name of Orville. Every time I said the name, we
laughed. By the time I got to the review itself, we were hysterical.
It was a book about a little boy who locked himself in his room all
day during the battle of Bunker Hill because he didn't want to die,
and Orville didn't like it.

"Orville!" I said.

"Borville!"

"Corville!"

"Dorville!"

We laughed! Then our laughing got weaker and quieter, until we were just sitting there across from each other, sort of giggling every once in a while. We'd forgotten about the television set and the football game when, all of a sudden, they were there. The room was getting dark, and there were men in uniforms running around, crashing into each other. Then the announcer said there was two minutes to go. And outside our window, I was sure I heard an airplane.

"Tired?" Jane said.

I said, "Yes."

"I wonder," Jane was turning her glass in her hands as she spoke, "I wonder if, when adults go to bed, whether they, if they undress in *front* of each other or — like one is in the bathroom and the other in the bedroom."

"Adults?" I said.

"Yes."

"I guess they just undress."

"Just in front . . . Together."

"Sure."

"They wouldn't worry about anything."

"I mean — if they're adults . . ."

"Uh-huh."

"You know."

"That's what I thought," she said.

"Sure."

"I was just — wondering."

"I guess it's sort of the *difference*."

"I know," Jane said. She finished her glass and set it on top of the television. There was the sound of a gun, and the announcer said that the game was all over. It seemed, all of a sudden, that there was an awful lot of shouting. Then none.

We undressed very quietly. The room was quite dark, and different colors of light from outside moved along the walls. There was one very large red patch that I watched the whole time. Finally, nothing was left for us but to stand and look at each other.

Jane broke the silence. "That's what being circumcised is, isn't it?" she said.

I told her, "Yes."

"That's interesting," she said. There was another silence. "Is it because you're Jewish?"

"I used to think so." Jane, undressed, was very beautiful. "An older kid told me once if I went into a men's room and there was someone there who hated Jews and he saw me that he might kill me. I used to wet my pants at school a lot because of it."

"Then what *is* the reason?"

"Health — that's what I heard later."

"Oh."

What surprised me most about Jane, naked, was the largeness and darkness of her nipples. I had thought that was true only of older women. But I didn't ask her.

"Orville," I said. Then we both started to laugh.

Jane said, "Let's take a shower."

I wanted to hug her but was afraid that without the clothes between us it would be cold.

We went into the bathroom, leaving the light off, and turned on the water. When it was good and warm, we stepped inside the curtain with two of those small hotel cakes of soap. While we were soaping each other all over, we got on another Orville kick. Then the soap kept slipping out of our hands, and we'd bump into each other every time we bent to pick it up.

We must have been in the shower, scrubbing and laughing, for about half an hour, maybe an hour. We used up every ounce of soap. It was like some preparation.

Drying each other wasn't as much fun. It was a little cold and it took me a long time to dry Jane's beautiful hair. Then, just like that, she ran out of the bathroom into the other room. It confused me. I just stood for a couple of minutes, stood where I was just holding the towel. I checked my teeth. They were pretty clean.

When I finally stepped through the bathroom door, I got a pillow flat across the face. I heard Jane scream with laughter, saw her, and hurled the pillow back. Then I got the other one in the stomach. Our laughing was the worst yet. Those pillows kept flying back and forth across the room. We missed; we hit each other; we knocked over a lamp. Back and forth they flew, like some crazy fat birds or planes.

At last, one of the pillows broke against the wall, and all the feathers came floating down over the floor and covers of the bed. It was so funny that I fell down onto the bed from laughing. Then, the next thing I knew, Jane was pounding me with the other pillow, laughing just as hard as I was. I grabbed it, and we started to fight for it. She was really strong, and I couldn't get the darn thing away from her.

"Orville," I said.

"Forville."

"Gorville!"

We were laughing, rolling around, still fighting for the pillow. Then, all of a sudden, it wasn't funny any more. We weren't fighting. The pillow fell aside someplace, and we didn't, couldn't, care. There was just us on the bed with the feathers all around, as if we'd plucked them from each other. Jane was making noises, funny noises. It was tangled. We were reaching. The covers weren't even over us; there were just the feathers. And we were reaching for each other all over, finding. Jane's hair was everywhere. Then all of it: the wildness, the feathers, the sounds, the lights blinking in colors outside our window, the feeling of explosion took us completely. That was all.

I woke from dreams of jets crashing, burning in midair. Jane was still sleeping face down beside me. She looked gray-white and sort of damp. Quietly, I slipped from the bed, picked up my clothes and went into the bathroom to dress. I wanted to shower again, but there was no soap; we'd used it all up.

Instead, I sat down on the toilet and tried very hard for relief. It didn't come. I must have sat there for half an hour trying, but it just wouldn't come. I'd left the light off, and when I stood up to dress, I hung a white towel over the mirror.

When I was dressed, suit, vest, everything, I turned on the light, took the towel from the mirror, and combed my hair. It was a cheap hotel. The mirror made your eyes seem to be everywhere but on either side of the bridge of your nose. And even the hot water was rusty.

I heard the television set go on in the room. It was the Saturday night fights, and I was surprised at the time's being so late. When I went through the door, I saw Jane sitting where she'd been at the very first, all dressed, even her camel's hair coat and her mittens and her scarf.

I didn't say anything; I just watched her for a while. I don't even remember who was fighting, but one of them was really getting it, just hanging onto the ropes. Jane was really watching hard, I walked over a little bit toward her.

"Hi."

She didn't even turn from the set. "I think he's going to fall," she said, almost whispering. "I think he's going to be knocked out."

"Janie?"

"Look at that!" she said. The fighter, a Negro in white trunks, slipped from the ropes onto the matting and the referee began to count. "Is he knocked out?"

I didn't answer.

"Arnold? Is he really hurt badly?" She still hadn't turned around.

"Probably."

"Does one man ever kill another?"

"Sometimes."

Seeing her from behind, it seemed that she must be smiling. I walked over and turned off the set. "Let's go," I said.

"It's late, isn't it?"

"We . . . Yeah, it must be about 11:30." We left, walked down the maroon hallway, entered the elevator and rode down, both of us, I think, listening to it creak. Then we walked out through the maroon lobby under the dull yellow light of the six chandeliers. When we got outside, I asked Jane if she'd like something to eat.

"That's all right, Arnold," she said. "I'll just take a cab or something. Mummy's probably worried."

"Aren't you hungry?"

"Yes, a little bit, but . . ."

"C'mon."

We walked west and found that the Calico Kitchen on Lexington Avenue was still open. Both of us had cheeseburgers and mocha sodas. We loaded our cheeseburgers with onions just in case the vodka should smell, a *lot* of onions — as if they were medicine or something. And while we ate, *both* of us, we just looked around or listened to each other chew. When we were through, still without a word, we got up and left.

Outside, it was awfully cold. Jane wrapped the scarf tight around her, and we walked east again. The walking was fast, almost like a race. When we got to the I.R.T. uptown, Jane said "Bye, Arnold," using only a flicker of a smile.

Before she could leave, I said, "I want to see something."

"What?"

"If the onions worked. Breathe!"

She breathed, and even in the cold air, the onions came across and made my eyes water.

"O.K.?"

"O.K. Try me." I breathed.

"O.K."

We breathed for each other again to make sure. I guess the onions we'd eaten were extra strong, because we stood in the subway entrance and there was water streaming out of both our eyes. It was almost as if we were crying.

Then for a minute we both almost smiled. It was so tiny and so weak. Then it stopped. We just couldn't. It wouldn't even have been funny if I'd said "Orville."

Suddenly I remembered. "Janie, where is it?"

"Where's what?"

"The wishbone. From the turkey."

She reached into the pocket of her camel's hair coat, fished around, and came out with the bone — broken. We both looked at it, the water from the onions drying on our faces.

"I wonder who would have won," I said.

"I wonder," Jane said.

"I really wonder," I repeated, and the onions were working again. We looked at each other.

It ended. She threw the pieces out into the street, turned, ran down into the subway and disappeared. Once again, I tried very hard to remember her, this time *with* the coat and the blond hair. But for the second time in less than two months, the picture failed.

The broken wishbone was lying in the street, and I went to pick it up. I bent down, then straightened up again and walked back to the subway. It really didn't make any difference *who* might have won. We *both* would have. I knew our wishes were the same.

There was a little change left in my pocket; so I took the subway up to 238th Street and the George Washington Bridge. I don't know why, but when I stepped from the train, I felt like running, and I ran up all the stairs to the street. Then I ran past a lot of buildings. And I ran by some people and they yelled something after me. I could see the bridge, and I ran toward it. There was a fence that I had to climb over and a banking I had to run down. I ran right across the West Side Highway without even looking. There were a lot of cars, but somehow none of them hit me. Then I could smell the river, and I stopped and looked up.

There were lights going back and forth over the water, lights without cars. I could see them shining in and out of the steel beams and disappearing into the huge concrete supports. I really don't know how long I stayed there, just looking up, watching the lights, but there was almost sun in the sky when I turned to leave. And I knew, I *knew* that all the while, all the long while I stood there, that there wasn't one plane, not one single plane in the whole, huge sky.

Marianna

The flowers, the sugar bowl, the teak-handled spoons, the cock-tail napkins, the thin plate of bakery cookies sat like a still life on the glass-topped coffee table. Marianna stood by the small sink slicing lemons, listening to a song on the portable stereo she had brought from home: "I am a maid," the song announced. The record circled. Marianna stood silent with a small paring knife clamped against the bright yellow rind, following the words: "I am a maid . . . of constant sorrow." The small apartment room droned — or was it cars passing outside on the Cambridge street? — droned with doubt, its air smelling thickly of citrus and of fall flowers.

In addition to the stereo, she had brought most of her books from home, all the paperbacks. She had left the *Oxford Book of English Verse* that her mother, at graduation, had inscribed: "A Woman's Garden of Verses. For your wisdom. All my love, Mother." She had left it with the *Collier's Encyclopedia* on her bedroom shelf. Some books were new, new since her coming; she liked those best, bought from the Paperback Gallery in the Square: the De Sade, Fromm, the books by Karen Horney, the novel that had so disturbed her — about the girl, like herself, leaving home; how awfully and overwhelmingly anonymous she had become or seemed to, instead of . . . The whole book had made her feel pasty, melted together, late one night when she'd read it.

So there was the stereo. And the books. And one of the lamps and the two-coil hotplate, and some dishes — "throwaways," her mother called them: "I'll never use them." But the bright pillows and the kitchen stool and the second-hand convertible couch that the Good Will men had carried up themselves and had taken the apartment door off and put it back on again to get in — all were new. And that accounted for everything. That made up the furnishings that she, at the age of nineteen, had lived with by herself for a week now. Marianna resumed her slicing and cut herself on the small paring knife.

"Shi — !" she stopped herself, thinking her mother might be outside waiting, listening, incredulous, unsure whether she had approached the right door, climbed the right flight of stairs. She had put her name on the mailbox, misspelling it somehow the first time, then getting it right; certainly her mother would see that. Warm blood, a bright bead of it, washed her fingertip like watercolor and the spot stung. Marianna ran the tap over it, hot before cold, and stood there distractedly feeling inadequate. She looked at the sake cups and jug on the counter and wondered if her mother would notice that they were not tea things. They were *modern*, she would tell her mother if the question came up; they were *modern*, that's all.

Marianna thought she heard a knock on the door and turned the tap off. She listened. It sounded again, and this time she heard — soft, hesitant, refined — her mother's hand. She touched her own damp fingers to her blouse to dry them, slipped the lemon slices on a small plate, a saucer, flipped on the hotplate burner under the teakettle, and stood. Still. She stood still and quiet to possess herself, to center that . . . shadow, that shifting breath called "Marianna" in herself; then she moved slowly, so as not to dislodge it, toward the door. But the knock, slight as it was, starting once more, jumbled her.

Her mother stood in the hall carrying packages, looking, in the split second before she smiled at her daughter, as Marianna had seen her look in museums or touring a new city.

"Oh . . ." her mother sighed gently. "Thank goodness."

"Hi," Marianna greeted her. There was a smudge, a small quirk of a smile that was hers. "Come on in. Inside."

"I wasn't sure," her mother said — started to say — but Marianna, backing away from the door, shied her from comment.

Marianna turned the record off; "I was just listening to music," she said. She picked up a case and slipped the record into it. She became aware that, even here, she was picking up her room.

"It's sweet," her mother said. "Oh, Marianna, it's sweet. It's very sweet. Really." She closed the door. "It is."

Marianna moved behind her mother. "Let me take your coat," she said.

"I had no idea it would be so sweet, really. One would never know from the hallway out there. I wasn't sure I was in the right place. But it's so sweet. You've made it look just lovely."

Marianna had her mother's coat; she draped it over her arm, but did not know what to do with it. "Well, there's a lot of things I want to do, but . . ." She looked around. Had she moved into an apartment without a closet? Was that possible? She'd been living out of her suitcase, on which the telephone now stood, for the week.

"It's cheery. Yes." Her mother wandered around, strolled, visibly struggling to show appreciation. "White walls. White walls — it makes the place look bigger. Did you paint . . . ?"

"No. It came that way. *They* did, I mean." Marianna nodded and wished for a closet.

"It was cute of you to think of inviting me for tea. Sweet and cute. I loved it. Daddy did too. Something burning?"

"Oh, God — here!" She handed the coat back to her mother, rushed to the hotplate to brush a smoking potholder onto the floor.

"Step on it," her mother offered. Marianna broke from her stance, her dismay, and stood, shifting feet waifishly on the smoldering patch. "That's it," her mother said finally, "I think you can pick it up and put it in the sink now." Marianna complied.

"It's really so sweet," her mother went on, crossing over, walking the small space again, setting her coat down on the end of the couch.

"I turned the wrong burner on," Marianna apologized.

"I do that." Her mother smiled; Mariana could almost feel the smile cross the room and pat her on the head.

"When?" she asked.

"I do that all the time. Who's that?" her mother questioned, pointing to an unframed print taped to the wall.

"Modigliani," Marianna said, her mother's ignorance settling her, giving her suddenly a pleasant and mild authority here in her own space, her own geometry of walls. She turned the burner on under the kettle, stood aware of herself and of the coil which she smelled heating.

"Oh, yes," her mother said, moving closer to it. "The neck. And Renoir — does the apple cheeks. They're nice. They're colorful. They're nice in here. They fit."

"Yes," Marianna said, nodding, "why don't you sit down?"

"Thank you. Oh . . . !" Her mother moved to the packages she had brought. "This one's for you."

"Mother."

"Apartment-warming!"

"Mother, I . . ."

"It's not charity."

"I know."

"Of course you do. It's done. It's always done whenever somebody moves into a new place. And it doesn't make any difference whether it's a mansion or a . . . room, a small apartment. Like this. Open it. Maybe you can't even use them. I don't know."

"Thank you." Marianna shrugged and looked sheepish. "Thank you."

"Open it." Her mother pulled the hem of her knit dress taut and smooth. She pinched a lint thread, held it between two thin fingers. "Do you need a vacuum?" her mother asked.

"I'm getting one." Marianna took the package, shook it slightly and smiled. Her mother smiled; the habit of shaking presents was hers: a gesture, a warm gesture of levity Marianna had learned. "Not a rattle," Marianna said.

"Not this time." Her mother, settled on the couch, took out a cigarette and lit it. Marianna fumbled with the wrapping. "Where do you study?" her mother asked.

"What?" Marianna was reading the card.

"Where do you study? . . . Your work."

"For your moveable feast," the card said. Marianna set it

aside. "Very nice," she spoke quietly and to the card.

"Do you know what it means? 'Moveable feast?' "

"I'll find out."

"Your school work," her mother pressed on; "where do you do that?" Now there was a smile and a careful ingenuousness about her question.

"Well . . ." Marianna was trying to peel the scotch tape without ripping the glossy orange paper. "I plan to get a desk." The kettle whistled. She left the package and moved across to the hotplate. "I've been using the library this week, but I plan to get a desk." She switched the burner off.

"Well, maybe the library's the best place." Her mother was looking for a place to put her ashes.

Marianna stood absorbed in the kettle's note, feeling the arc of it hold and then fade. The sound contained all the private pleas, the birdlike outbursts, the wan moments of madness — there, tiny, then gone; pressure and release. They thinned with the steam, the song, then pared themselves — more than sighs, less than shrieks — steadily into muteness. Marianna, reaching for the handle, relaxed.

"Ash . . . ?" Her mother stopped herself. "How late is the library open?" she asked instead.

"What?" Marianna had forgotten that the room was occupied.

"I was wondering what hours you were putting in there. Well, actually, I was wondering what time you were in transit, coming home. What time of night. I mean, the neighborhood . . . Well, I know you can take care of yourself; it's not that." She stopped herself again. "Well, actually, I don't know what I was saying, I guess." A second ash, rod-like, dropped from its own weight onto the floor. "But I do hate to dirty up your floor," her mother said, holding her cigarette straight up.

"That's all right."

Marianna held the tea kettle in one hand, steadying the sake jug with the other.

"If you had a . . ."

"Just a minute, Mother!" she said, feeling her right hand begin to tremble. Her mother bowed her head slightly and drew silent. She pinched the cigarette out on her shoe, put the butt in her purse, then rubbed her thumb and first fingers together in a mild finicky gesture.

Steam from the tea water, a thin rivulet falling unbrokenly into the sake jug, diffused in front of Marianna's eyes, moistening them. She was afraid she'd lose her concentration, her focus, but the jug filled and she set the kettle back on the hotplate without mishap.

"What were you saying?" Marianna asked; "I'm sorry."

"Nothing."

"No, really; I didn't mean to interrupt you." As she spoke, she rummaged for teabags in the small single wall cabinet someone had painted blue.

"Nothing. I forgot — really," her mother said. "Really."

Marianna remembered she had laid the tea bags out, four of them, the strings taut to the tag, in case they had two cups apiece. They were there, ready, on the counter, like pajamas laid out on her bed at home.

"What lovely spoons!" Her mother pressed toward a lightness.

"Yes. Thank you." Marianna forced the thick teabags into the small sake cups. "There's a shop," she said abstractedly, "in the Square."

"Wood handles!"

"Teak," she said. "Those are teak."

"Oh, yes. Teak. Lovely spoons. Stylish."

Marianna wondered if there was any room left in the cup for water. If the teabag swelled, it would fill the cup. Maybe she should break one teabag and divide the leaves.

"Need some help?" Her mother shifted on the couch and smiled.

"No. No, thanks." Marianna poured the water from the sake jug into the cups. The teabags, rising, nearly floated out, but with a churchkey and some spilling she stuffed them back again and, waterlogged, they stayed. The water stained, took on a deep mahogany. Marianna's phone rang.

"Oh . . . !" her mother said, starting, not somehow anticipating phone sounds in this place.

Marianna picked up the two cups, burning her left index finger where she had cut it with the paring knife, put them on a thin breadboard, carried them over to the coffee table and set them down.

"I'm sorry," she said to her mother. "I'll get it. I'll be right with you." Her mother looked down at the tiny cups, the board, ran her tongue over her lips, but said nothing.

With one hand on the receiver, Marianna moved away from the suitcase tabling its base. Unlike the long extension at home, this cord was coiled short and springy, and Marianna, trailing it, had not, herself, made the adjustment yet. The base clattered to the floor. Her mother winced, nearly jumped.

"I'm sorry," Marianna said to whoever it was. "Oh — oh, hi." Her mother moved and picked up the base, setting it back. They smiled at each other, both nervously, before her mother, almost apologetically, withdrew and sat once more on the couch, considering her tea.

"Well . . ." Marianna continued, that thing, that "Marianna" thing she had wanted so much to possess, caught in the brambles of a pause. She glanced over at her mother. Her mother received the glance and, losing herself in caution, picked up her cup. "Well, I'm not sure," Marianna went on. There was a pause. Her mother, leaning way forward, nibbled hurriedly at her tea. "No, just not sure."

Carefully, from the neat plate, her mother took a thin cookie, took a small bite from it and stood. Marianna, listening but noticing, wrinkled her brow.

"I have to run," her mother whispered, picking up her coat, offering a smile, this time her woman's substitute for a wink.

Marianna, still listening, shook her head *no*. "What? — I'm sorry," she said, but at her mother shook her head more insistently. "What?"

"Supper," her mother said, softly again, slipping on her coat.

"Uhhh . . ." Marianna filled a telephone pause, stamping her foot to get her mother's attention. "Listen," she said to whoever it was, "could I call . . . Could I call you . . . ?" They were exchanging hand gestures now, her mother's *don't worry about me*: two hands open and vertical: half pacification, half benediction. And Marianna's *don't be stupid*: single sharp strokes of an open hand, like someone trying to tell a car that it's backing into a parking space too fast. "Listen, I'll call you back." And she hung up. "What are you doing?" she asked her mother. "Where are you going?"

"Well," and she did her best to produce a twinkle, "I have a home too," her mother said and smiled.

"But we were going to have tea. Here. I didn't even have a chance to ask you if you took lemon or anything."

"Nothing."

"Or cream."

"Nothing — I took it that way. It was good. Thank you."

"But . . ."

"Plenty of time."

"Well, yes, but . . ."

Her mother was adjusting a small hat Marianna had not even noticed her wearing. "I just wanted to see where you were. How you were. How everything was. And now that I know I can find my way, of course I'll be back."

"Well, I just thought today . . ."

"Plenty of time."

The two drifted toward the door nearly dancing — steps, motion, selves quite like complements.

"Daddy all right?"

"Fine. Says 'hello.' "

"Yes — well . . ."

"It's so sweet, really," her mother said, looking around again. "It is." And then she added, "It's so nice to see you acting so independently like this."

"Well, there are still a lot of things that have to be done,"

Marianna said, "but . . ."

Her mother touched her hand, then the handle of the door. "That's always true," she said. "I'll give your love to Daddy."

"Yes," Marianna said, standing with her. "I'll have you both up for supper some night. It's not that far."

"That would be nice." Her mother leaned forward and kissed her. She called her by a name she had not called her for fifteen years. "Goodbye, Memi," she said gently.

"Goodbye," Marianna echoed quietly.

"Thank you so much."

"Yes."

"It was lovely."

"Well . . . there are still an awful lot of things I want to do, but . . ."

They exchanged smiles. The door shut. Marianna could hear the progress of her mother down the hall, then on the stairs, footfalls without either haste or hesitation, and she could smell her mother's mild scent, wondering in this small room if it might stay there now for several days. Marianna smelled her own flesh, her skin, the back of her hand to see if she had her own scent any more. There was scent of lemon there, she could smell, and of tea, but of herself, of Marianna, no, she could not be sure. She felt her eyes cloud and leaned against the door.

It was after five, with long shadows in the room from the light through the single window, and the objects — spoons, napkins, cookies, flowers — seemed more composed and unreal than they had less than half an hour before. Marianna put some Bach on the stereo to play softly, then realized she had never opened her mother's gift.

It was a tea set: china, Rosenthal. Marianna broke one of the cups, then set the pieces out carefully, almost like a flower, on a cocktail napkin, so that tomorrow, after she bought the Elmer's Glue she discovered she did not have, she could, she hoped, make repairs.

Little Sister

When Caroline Nelson boarded the afternoon bus for Sandusky, her total outfit consisted of a woven Navajo bag, a gold V-neck sweater, bell-bottom levis, a pair of calf-length black imitation leather boots, a string of dull amber plastic beads, a scrap of newspaper bearing the brief account of her father's recent morals conviction and $8.32 in one-dollar bills and change. It was July, 1969. She was thirteen years of age, bright, timid, and marked by the illusions, if not the ignorance, of youth.

She paid her fare and almost immediately felt herself noticed — flat-chested and frail. She smiled defensively to herself and for whoever might be appraising her, then sat. She watched the Ohio summer dinginess go by and felt middle-aged. She watched the outskirt houses, copies of her own, unsightly, like green asbestos patches at the edges of cornfields: the inadequate shade of their one or two trees, the stripped wheelless cars, the disabled hayracks, the crippled flat-back trucks, the tire swings, the small scruffy dogs scratching up dust, the broken fences and the anemic ponies which, again like her own — gone in February — were either standing dead or would pass away soon. And she could almost smell the bird droppings on everything: dull, calcified, the mockery of magpies and swallows in the dry heat.

But soon — not even the length of a daydream in which she swam nude with a boy who looked like Peter Fonda at the second Woodstock Festival — soon all of this gave way to tract houses and shopping centers, enormous revolving marquees boasting chicken at sixty-nine cents a pound, stores barricaded with bags of charcoal. And then, just as swiftly, there was Sandusky — no gaps, building set against building, all gaining, all growing, *up*, as they neared Lake Erie, *up*, none of them very glamorous. But Carrie didn't care. She took a small pin from her levi pocket and worked a place on her arm, a reddish mark. She told her friends here — Darlene, Steve, and Phil — that she was shooting speed. The sting from the small pin made her eyes blear.

The bus docked, and passengers, mostly in summer cottons and shirt sleeves, filed out. Carrie waited to see if anything was left, forgotten, things she might use. Only the flattened half of an Almond Joy, lodged in a seat crevice, offered itself and she took that, eating it quickly, wiping the moist chocolate from her fingers on the back of a seat.

Carrie went to the terminal counter and got coffee. Sometimes her friends were there, using the station to hit on grass or pick up some stranger's unwatched suitcase. They were all fifteen or sixteen.

There were crumbs baked by dishwater heat into her saucer and Carrie felt them with her finger. Had she nails, she might have dug them off. She drank her coffee slowly while a man in a tentish and gray lightweight suit kept his eyes on her. He thought she was a whore, she imagined — though she had never seen a whore. And she kept wetting her lips with her tongue while she drank and kept looking at him from the corner of her eye. The whole pantomime excited her, until he asked, weirdly she thought, for the sugar, which she passed abruptly. Then left.

Outside, the Sandusky street warmth seemed more drying than usual. It seemed fresh. Carrie's arms and face felt like she imagined towels felt in the laundromat, right from the dryer, lying folded on the top of some wicker basket. She took her boots off and moved toward a coffeehouse, The Icarus, walking lazily, tracking some sort of purposeful high along the sidewalk for the businessmen on the street all to watch. She hit people for quarters when she thought she could. "Watch their eyes," her friend Steve had told her. "Some of them love it. If they're watching you: hit. It's the price of admission." When she got to The Icarus, she had $2.25 more. And that pleased her. And she thought: I can live on panhandling here. Maybe waitress. I can live with Darlene, *meet* people. Then, when I have enough put together, move on. Kids pass through.

She had heard talk about Haight and the East Village. Lots — lots of kids. Dangerous too, she'd heard said. Dangerous, well maybe, but nothing could hit harder than her mother when she'd been drinking. So . . . And besides — wasn't that right? yes it was — besides, as long as she stayed in Ohio, *anywhere*, anywhere in Ohio, even Sandusky, she would just go on feeling like a bug. It was just a matter of money, then — and the right time.

No one was at The Icarus. The manager had no idea where her friends might be. So Carrie ordered a lemon coke, sat down and waited, did her "waiting performance." She had a baggie in her Navajo purse. It was filled with pills which she'd taken from medicine cabinets in almost every bathroom she'd ever visited. Most were, of course, aspirin. So she took the baggie, held it up for a while, let the sun play through the plastic and around its folds, gathered an audience. Then she reached in and took, one at a time, holding each up for some sort of vague inspection, four of the pills, dropping them from a good height into her coke. Then she sat — and drank slowly, drank until she brought about a dim, giggling high, carefully directing it in her mind. Carrie loved making scenes.

She loved being at the center of them. No one had ever noticed her in Vickery except to shout or hit at until a month and a half ago, until just after eighth-grade graduation. She'd been a pencil, an inkwell, a tile in the corridor. No teacher had even asked her to stay after school. No boy had ever taken her up in the balcony at the Capitol or to the afternoon parties at McGiver's abandoned chickenhouse. But meeting Darlene that Saturday in late May on her "graduation present day" in Sandusky had changed things.

Well — not really with boys, though. And she wasn't sure she wanted that changed anyway. She had had dreams of herself and her father — at least she had relegated them to dreams; they had happened at confused centers of dark nights — which disturbed her. She had woken up bruised. And, for some reason, she was not a girl, before or now, who could imagine herself ever having children, even womanly breasts. Oh, she'd been naked with boys here in Sandusky, swimming and dancing around, but that wasn't anything. That was fun.

But now, with her pill-doctored coke, here at The Icarus, she was noticed, at the middle of some circle, like an important point, like the prick a compass makes on paper when it draws perfectly round things; that dot through which, when you hold the paper up, the light from outside the windows always shines. Like a star. And a much older couple, *much* older, several tables away, was watching her. So she took a sugar cube from the bowl in front of her and unwrapped it — for some effect: giggling, singing to herself, imagining herself Janis Joplin high on acid. And when the manager walked over as she thought he might and asked her to leave, calling her "more hippie jailbait," she thought it was a great phrase, and she kept repeating it, drifting a dramatic path to the door, envisioning herself — somewhere; at some future, though not really *too* future time — a great, nationally-discussed actress.

What to do now? The city light seemed thicker now: baked, like illuminated concrete, and it quieted her. She seemed to lose her life for a while, to be shuttled back again six months to the time she felt like an object: a candy wrapper in a doorway, a lid tab from a beer or soft-drink can in her splotched, weedy yard that no one would ever possibly attend to. Carrie found herself crying, her eyes running quietly.

She loved cream. Cream made things better. It was a child's taste and habit; she understood that, but it lingered, and so to lift and mellow herself, she bought a pint of cream and sat in a small green park, drinking it, sucking sugar cubes from The Icarus. And things seemed better. A little. There was still a low buzz of memories, yes, and fears, and Carrie grew anxious for ways to displace them, for her friends, for things to do. So she went and stole a brightly colored silk scarf and tied her hair in it.

Then she found Phil moving deliberately along the street.

"We're going to New York!"

"New *York*!"

"Darlene, Steve, and me."

"*All?*" Carrie asked.

"Yeah," he grinned, "it's crazy!"

"Wow."

"Total freak!"

"Would you . . . ?" Carrie watched Phil's eyes shadow over.

"What."

"Take me?"

"What about your parents?"

"Zero. I've left."

"No kidding?"

"Yeah."

"When."

"Today."

"This morning?"

"Yeah. They don't know. They don't know anything. It won't make any difference anyway. Except maybe to my sister, Janine. Maybe to her. But . . ." Carrie's mind skipped, then grabbed hold again. "I *want* to go. Let me. See, I was going *any*way. In a week or so. I'd *planned* it."

"Yeah?"

"Yeah."

"On what?"

"Bread!"

"How much?"

"Ten. Maybe eleven. If I handle some this afternoon, I can get maybe five more. I know it."

Phil paused. He looked at her as though he were watching a ripped grocery sack, or a stalled car engine or something. "Meet us back here by three," he finally told her. "We want to get to New York by morning. Use rides for sleeping."

"Thanks," Carrie said.

"We won't wait," Phil said almost regretfully, then moved off.

By three Carrie had $7.20 more. She had managed to hit six people for $1.20 busfare in that time. She had done it by crying, crying nearly the whole hour, and when she met her friends, her face looked as though it had been crumpled, then unfolded. There were forty-year-old creases on it. And lines.

"$17.37! I've got $17.37 altogether!"

Her friends each had more. They'd been planning it.

"Better do it in couples," Steve announced. "Me and Darlene. Phil, you and Carrie."

Carrie looked at Phil. Phil looked at Steve, then down at the pavement. There was a half-rotation of his jaw. "O.K. — O.K. We'll take first ride," he said. Then looked up.

Steve nodded to him. "Meet in Washington Square Park."

A Mustang took them only about a mile and a half to where they connected with a red Volkswagen which took them out of city limits, onto a state highway and nearly all the way to an Ohio Turnpike interchange. And when the driver — soft, muted, and friendly, like his car — bought them supper at a small roadside restaurant, they told him they'd both just been dropped from their summer jobs without severance and were trying, somehow, to make it back to New York.

"Where do you live?"

"On the East Side," Phil said.

"Down in the Village," Carrie added. And Phil looked at her like she'd just spilled mustard on his new corduroy flair pants.

When they left the VW driver, it was almost dark. And they put their thumbs out on the Ohio Turnpike against a traffic that seemed to be fleeing east from an Illinois on fire, all the engines thirsting for night. The couple was barely visible in the dark; it was nearly two and a half hours before anyone stopped.

They caught a small independent meat truck going straight to the city. Carrie felt happy. The man said he supplied a half-dozen restaurants there. Carrie had to ride in the semi-refrigerated back with the meat, because there was only room for one in the cab with the driver — and Phil took that. She was cold. It was night, and there was no light in the van and she felt chilled in the darkness there with the heavy smell of the meat which she could almost hear breathing in thick shapes all around her. Why hadn't Phil let her ride in the cab — on his lap or squeezed beside him? She couldn't understand.

So Carrie found a space on the moist floor and tried to curl, pulling into herself, gathering warmth. She could sense the dangling beef and hung chickens above her now, could sometimes make them out, swaying lightly with the fixed rhythm of the truck. She shut her eyes. She thought of the kitchen in Vickery, thought of the refrigerator packed with beer quarts. She thought of the dozens of plastic containers: seven peas and three wedges of carrot in one, a teaspoonful of mashed potato in another, four wax beans in a third — food, all of which would eventually get thrown out. It was the plastic containers, not the leftovers, her mother loved to make use of. Then Carrie fell asleep.

The rear doors of the van clanged and woke her. She could hear the traffic whining up and past.

"Carrie . . . ?" Phil called softly in to her. She could see his outline. He sounded at the end of a school corridor.

"Are we there?" she asked sleepily, still on the floor. She thought of the enormous city. She became excited.

"C'mere!" His voice was serious. "I have to talk to you."

She got up and crawled out and through the door. It was much warmer outside. "Are we almost there?" She could see they were still on some highway.

"Listen . . ." He looked concerned. "Listen, the guy *told* me something. The driver."

"What?"

"He said that he and I could get in a lot of trouble taking you across a state border. He said we could be arrested. Put in jail."

"What do you mean?"

"I mean it's against the law to be with a girl, a girl your age, and then take her from one state to another."

The sleep was clearing from Carrie's head now; she was warming. "But you're not *taking* me."

"He said I *am*."

"What do you mean?"

"I mean, you got to go the rest of the way by yourself."

"Phil . . . !"

"I'm serious."

"But how will I . . . ?"

"We'll wait for you in Washington Square. What Steve said. Washington Square. Find Washington Square. There's a fountain there. Steve said. That's where we'll be."

She was beginning to shake. She heard the driver's voice from the front of the truck call "Hey!" and "Come on!" to Phil, saw Phil nod.

"See you there." He moved ahead.

The side door opened. She watched the exhaust color yellow and then red in the tail lights; saw the truck pull out, leaving her.

Carrie had no idea where she was, no idea of time. There were only the sound and the briefly-lit impression of cars streaking by. And she could still smell meat, feel the dampness of the blood on her sweater and levis where she'd lain. Carrie had never thumbed a ride by herself before. I'll get a ride fast though, I'm sure; she tried to bolster herself with that thought.

She stood by the side of the highway for an hour, perhaps more, the bravado she had gained in the last month and a half drained by each passing set of lights. Finally, a car stopped, a new GTO. There were two girls in the front; a rack solid with clothes hung across the back. Carrie felt hope again — and relieved.

"Where're you going?" the girl not driving asked her.

"New York," Carrie said sheepishly. "City."

"Hop in," the girl said. "Back! Squeeze the dresses."

Carrie opened the back. She would make it! She crawled along the seat until she was in, then closed the door. She parted the clothes like curtains somewhere near the middle and put her head and shoulders into the space as the car squealed out into the traffic lane and both girls in front laughed.

"You freaking out?" the girl who had spoken before, a blonde, asked her.

Carrie felt her face heat. "No. . . . I . . . No, I live there," she said softly. "I live there."

"Where've you been, then?" the driver asked.

"What?" Carrie tried to give herself time to think.

The two girls looked at each other and laughed. "Where — have — you — been?" the driver repeated, isolating each word.

"I . . . got let off a summer job. In Ohio," Carrie told her. "In Sandusky. Waitressing."

"That why you smell like hamburg?"

"I . . . *Do* I?"

"Yes."

"I don't know."

There was an uneasy span of silence. The two in the front looked at each other again and smiled.

"Listen — sweetheart — you at all interested in tricking for an International Syndicate of Whorehouses?"

Carrie could see them both fighting laughter. She felt like a button on one of the overhead rack dresses; like a hook, an eye, a snap on some pair of gloves.

". . . No."

"What?"

"Didn't catch that."

"No. I said, 'No.' . . . Thanks."

"Why? You still a virgin?"

Carrie was finding it hard to breathe. Maybe it was the lack of space, being stuffed in with all the hung cloth and material.

"What are you? How old, anyway? Eleven? Twelve?"

"I'm sixteen."

"And still a virgin?" It was the driver, back again, waiting out all of Carrie's held breath and stillness.

"Hey — she just asked you . . ."

"No!" Carrie shot the word out, and lied. "No. No, just not a . . . !"

The car broke suddenly to the side and stopped. The driver turned around and stared at Carrie. "O.K. — get out," she said.

"Why?" Carrie asked.

"Either say you're a whore — or get out."

Outside the car, traffic was thick; it was rushed and blurring. Carrie measured things. Both girls looked back at her, twin elbows on the seat back.

"Come on, Runaway!" the blonde said.

"Say it, Runaway."

Carrie told them what they wanted to hear.

"Thanks, honey."

"Thanks."

"We needed that."

"We both needed that."

"Needed to have it *out*."

"To have it *said*."

"Because it's reassuring."

They turned back. The car revved again, alive, and pulled away.

"We're all whores." The blonde lit a cigarette.

They both laughed, on and off, stealing looks at each other and into the rearview mirror at Carrie for almost twenty minutes. At one point they became almost hysterical. It was frightening.

But nothing else was said all the rest of the way to New York. There was only the sense of private voices playing under the car radio. At one point, the girls in front switched positions. Carrie slept fitfully. She woke up with the blonde's hand pressing her on the shoulder. "O.K.," the blonde said; "this is it."

Carrie got out. She felt her blood begin to buzz expectantly. She smelled damp stone and torn paper everywhere. She heard truck gears, people shouting in a foreign language. She felt thousands of miles away from Ohio and Vickery. "Thanks," she said.

"Think nothing of it," the blonde smiled.

"Just remember who you are," the driver added. And they pulled away.

Carrie asked eagerly and made her way to Washington Square Park. The others, she was sure, would be waiting. It was after

three-thirty in the morning. None of her friends, Steve, Phil, or
Darlene, were there by the fountain. There were drunks there,
sleeping. There were a man and a woman, both, Carrie thought,
terribly, terribly thin, sharing a cigarette. There was an older boy,
wearing a knapsack, playing quietly on his guitar; he had long red
hair and a red beard. A very thin black man came. He wore calf-
length boots. He sat down on the edge of the fountain, took one of
the boots off, emptied what seemed like a great quantity of blood
from it, slipped it on again, stood up and left. The boy playing the
guitar asked her to go have some coffee with him.

"I'm waiting here for some friends," she said.

"What are their names?"

"Steve and Phil and Darlene."

"I have a friend named Steve," the red-headed boy told her.
"I've got to have some coffee," he said, rose and left.

Two men walked by. One had a large burlap bag. The other
had a net. Carrie saw them move suddenly to one side, net a pigeon,
break its neck and throw it into the bag. She heard sirens somewhere. She heard garbage trucks. Two policemen crossed the park.
She saw them looking at her. It was getting light. The boy who
had left came back with a container of coffee for her.

When her friends hadn't come by 8:30, she agreed to spend
the day with the boy. She was excited to have met somebody. His
name was Durrant. He was from Salt Lake City, but he said he
knew New York very well. He bought her breakfast and talked to
her about a poet, Theodore Roethke. Carrie did not understand
most of what he said. He seemed to her to be very, very gentle, but
then at one point he said that he could very well assassinate Richard
Nixon. "You've got to deal with violence," he told her. "It's everywhere. Even in quiet people. It's the one really true thing to hold
on to." Carrie wasn't quite sure what he meant. But she liked him.

Durrant took her walking in Central Park. He talked about
another poet, Galway Kinnell. He offered her a joint. They shared
it. It was nice. Galway, Theodore, Durrant — why were all the
names here so strange? Durrant told her, "I like your breasts. I

don't think it's necessary for a girl to have enormous breasts."
Carrie felt funny. It was hard for her to think that she even *had*
breasts. She thought about her dog in Vickery — Candy — about
Candy lying in the shade of the old rust-spotted car frame in the
Nelsons' patchy backyard when she'd had puppies.

They had lunch. "I don't have any morey left. I spent it all
on breakfast," Durrant told her. "You'll have to buy me this."
The bill came to $3.28.

They went back to Washington Square, but none of Carrie's
friends were waiting there by the fountain. Durrant left her. "I
need to be alone," he said. "It just hit me. Good luck. Thanks for
lunch. I need to be alone."

"Sure," Carrie said to him.

"Do you know you've got blood on you?" Durrant asked.

"Oh," Carrie said. "Yes."

She stayed. She sat on the edge of the fountain there and
waited. Tonight her friends would find her! She watched some
children moving on the playground equipment, mothers sitting on
green benches to the side. She remembered playing with an old
breadbox in the field at the side of her house, playing with it in the
dry, dry Ohio sun, hiding stones and pieces of root and rusty spoons
and forks in it while her mother slept after her job. She remembered being outside, hearing the phone ring on and on and on
inside the house.

She noticed that a lot of people in the city had dogs.

A girl somewhat older than herself came over to her and asked
her if she wanted to crash.

"No. No, I'm waiting for some friends," Carrie said. The girl
stared a long time at her before she left. Carrie thought there was
something very cracked and dusty about the girl's eyes. It reminded
her of the wallpaper in her Ohio bedroom.

Carrie noticed more and more people watching her. Sometimes someone would cross the park, back and forth across the
square by the fountain, eyes on her all the time. She chased someone down who looked like Steve: "Steve . . . !" But it wasn't Steve.

After dark, she went to Chock Full O' Nuts and had some tomato soup and a chopped beef sandwich. She'd have to try to string her money out, she knew. No one was at the fountain when she got back.

She spent the night there. There was some sleep, but mostly Carrie drank a pint of cream she'd bought and searched out faces moving anywhere near her, studied them hopefully. She pretended to be stoned once, for an old man who was watching her, but she stopped when he started toward her. A boy, not much older than herself, kept appearing, sprinting the pathways. He was clutching a faded army blanket around him; it was all he seemed to have on. His eyes were huge, and he made sounds like tropical birds Carrie had seen once in the Toledo zoo.

The next day, Carrie took journeys out from the fountain into more of the city. It astonished her! At least a dozen people asked her if she knew she had blood on her, asked her if she was all right. She kept seeing what she thought were quite unusual sights: cats on leashes; an unplucked chicken leg on the sidewalk; a car, its windshield beaten in, stripped of wheels; dolls' arms and heads in the gutter.

That night a boy who said his name was Will stopped and talked to her. He kept nodding his head all the time as if he were listening to music. His girlfriend met him there: "Hey! This is Tracy," he told Carrie. "Tracy, this here is Carrie. Carrie's cool." Tracy and Will invited Carrie to a party in the Village, and she went there with them. She smoked a lot of dope and felt warm and good for the first time in a couple of days. She put on her crazy act: "Crazy Carrie." Darlene used to call her that. She met a boy named Sandy. "You're O.K.," Sandy told her, and she felt un-shrunk again. Sandy gave her more dope to smoke. She and Sandy went to an attic room in the apartment house, and it was unreal but she had her first sex with Sandy on some old curtains there. The party ended about two-thirty and she looked for Sandy, but he was gone. Everyone, it seemed, that she had met that night was gone; so she found her way back to Washington Square and the park.

Again she spent the night there, but none of her Sandusky friends came to find her. The next day she tried panhandling, but she got only a dollar and some pennies. Late in the afternoon, someone snatched her purse. That night, while she was waiting, someone else asked her to a party and she went and smoked more dope and let a boy named Robert have her in a closet. She forgot a little about being hungry that way. Then Robert brought a friend of his named Kim over to meet Carrie and a little later, she and Kim did the same thing in the same place. Kim asked her if she would like to try some heroin and she said no. And he said, "Come on; what the heck; just to do it; just to try it once." And Carrie told him, yes, she would, if he would take her out and buy her a hamburger and some french fries and a dish of ice cream. Kim said yes and they went to a place called Hungry Charley's, then came back, and Carrie tried some heroin and vomited everything she'd eaten.

She left the party and went over to the park, but a pair of policemen kicked her out. And so Carrie walked. She was incredibly hungry. She thought that she'd take some more heroin if it was offered to her, anything so that she didn't feel her body being so small, so raw and tired. She tried going back to the park but she saw the policemen still there. When it got light and people started passing her in more concentration on the streets, she panhandled another dollar and got herself a good breakfast and felt better. Today, she was sure, she'd find her friends.

She saw Kim late in the morning in the park. "Where'd you go last night?" he asked her.

"I just left."

"Wanta try some more stuff?"

"No thanks."

"Buy you another hamburg."

"No."

In the afternoon, Carrie watched a whore, a tiny woman with a red Afro, pick up a man near the Astor Place subway station. She followed them and found out where the nearby hotel was. Later on she picked a man up herself.

"How much?"

"Five dollars." She guessed.

The man was small and heavy and had mostly gray hair, and all Carrie could look at were his bad, terribly stained teeth. The minute it was over, she ran for at least five or six blocks, ran to get away. The street seemed littered with broken teeth.

She ate again. She kept it down. But she began to feel her clothes, the dirt in them and in her skin. She smelled herself. She still smelled like the back of the meat truck, that and the hotel room and the man and the party with Kim and Robert in the closet.

After dark she started asking people who passed the fountain if they had a place where she could go to shower and just wash her clothes. "I need to clean up," she would tell them. At last, a well-dressed man stopped and looked at her; he just stared. "Come on," he finally said.

The man was young, in his late twenties. They caught a cab and he took Carrie to where he lived, a large high-ceilinged apartment on the East Side. There were hundreds of old album-type brown photographs in small frames all over the walls and there were lots of crocks everywhere with tall seagrasses. Carrie showered. She washed her clothes in the tub. The man had wonderful-smelling soap and Carrie scrubbed and scrubbed herself and her clothes with it. She was in New York, she thought. She was living now in New York, New York City. She remembered her mother, standing by the screen door always in the late afternoon, drinking straight vanilla extract. She remembered her father, sitting on the toilet with the bathroom door wide open.

When Carrie went out into the apartment with a large towel wrapped around her, the man who had brought her there was listening to classical guitar music on his stereo, eating slices of avocado.

"My clothes are drying," Carrie told him. "I hung them up."

"You won't need them," the man said.

"Why?"

"Never mind why. Don't talk to me. I don't want to have to respond to you," the man said. He poured himself some red wine. "I just want to have you here. To watch."

He didn't touch her. But he didn't let her leave the apartment for three days. He told her that she could have any food that she wanted, but that she would have to cook it for herself. She could have her clothes later. She became scared and cried. She told him that she was an addict and needed heroin. He told her that that was unfortunate because he could not get her any. She screamed, and he watched her scream, listened to her, turned the guitar music up higher on his music system. Carrie would say things to him, but he would never answer her.

Late in the afternoon of the third day, the man said, "I think your clothes must be dry by now," and he rose from the chair he had been sitting in and undid all the locks and latches on his door. Carrie dressed and left.

No one resembling Steve or Phil or Darlene waited anywhere near the park. Two days later, Carrie met a boy named Peter, who was eighteen, and moved in with him. Peter was a sophomore at NYU. He wanted Carrie to cook for him. He shared his food with her, gave her wine and dope. A lot of Peter's friends came over, day and night, and they all talked about things that Carrie didn't understand. So on the fifth day she'd been with Peter, she took thirty dollars of his and left.

At the Howard Johnson's on Sixth Avenue she met a boy named Clark. Clark had a Triumph and he drove her out that afternoon to Long Island, and that night she moved in with him.

She lived with Clark for almost two weeks. He was only seventeen. His parents were very wealthy and they paid his rent. His apartment was much nicer than Peter's and Carrie didn't have to cook. Clark wanted her — he was frank about it — just to sleep with. "This is my Ohio runaway," he introduced her. Carrie tried heroin again with Clark and a friend of Clark's, Alan, and it was much better than it had been with Kim. On Thursday of the second week, though, she found the keys to Clark's Triumph, took it and sold it to a car dealer she found in Brooklyn for a thousand dollars. She had given up long ago on her Sandusky friends. She had never had so much money before in her life.

She bought clothes. She stayed three days in the New York Hilton. She put on weight. She drank cream. She found a bar that would serve her wine. She told nobody that she met that she was from Ohio. She met the leader of an acid rock group called the India Chutney, a boy named Alex, and moved in with him. He lived up on Second Avenue, high in an apartment house, with windows viewing the East River. Carrie did a lot more heroin with Alex and the group. She liked them. She understood what they talked about. She stole another sports car some commuter had left the keys in, drove it to Brooklyn and sold it for fifteen hundred.

Whenever Carrie was high, she used to think of the baked and dusty house in Vickery: the sere and tangled vines, the unmowed grass, her mother never answering the phone, the pony that her parents had let die, the bald tires and the burnt-up couch cushions left, overgrown, in the bushes. How far, she thought; how far she was from all of that right now. And she would look out and see the boats on the river, the late sun in reflected embers off the glass, the pigeons and waterbirds against the air, the smoke pictures — some of them like small animals — in the pink-gray of the sky. And she would smoke a joint, drink cream, eat a tangerine — she had grown to love tangerines — sit in the window chair, lean her face up against the cool surface of the glass, and float. Steam would start up from street grates, then dissolve. She would hitch rides on things: dim bands of music from car radios, dusk lights in rooms and on bridge cables. And there would be a sense in Carrie — there in her chair by her window, taking such trips — of phantom tenderness, such as she would never know.

The Frame Lover

There was this '53 Buick in Tom Harvey's Shell Station and it was for sale. One hundred and fifty bucks. I was fifteen years old — and seven months. I wanted it. I knew just how it was put together. I wanted to get in it. I loved the frame.

I made a deal. I didn't have any money (which was a problem) so I pumped gas nights, six to nine at the station, while Tom, the owner, went home to eat. This was seven years ago. On March eleventh that year, I turned sixteen. It was a snowy day, very snowy. Tom was late for work and I had gasoline soaked in my sneakers from the spill, but the work, the pumping, out in the snow with the gasoline smell swirling in my nose, had made me excited waiting for him, and when he came I took the keys for the first time, opened the door and got in. It was the start of what one person called an "obsession."

It was something! Everything around me — the whole world: the Shell station, the railroad tracks behind the station, the going-to-work traffic out on Concord Avenue — just kind of took off, passed away through the snow, went, and I had this unbelievable sense. It was of time. It was the sense of living forever, never being late for school, having no parents, just being, in a word I heard once, in "eternity," being inside eternity in the car. That was the one time I thought about myself as an artist, a great artist, thought that maybe I could paint anything, that possibly I had *seen* Jesus Christ and could paint him — just like *they* did, the great artists. At least paint birds.

The engine was pretty cold, I guess, not having been run for so long, and it didn't start. You could hear it trying. All the parts were there. The frame was strong. It just wouldn't start. Tom said he'd fix it up if I worked another month for him. That was

O.K. I still had to get my license anyway.

As it worked out, I pumped *three* more months. Tom said the car needed rings, pistons, valves, a new carb. I wanted to be good to it, wanted my frame to be happy, to be glad I was *in* it, *moving* it. So I pumped, and, even while Tom was doing the work, started buying things for it — some retread whitewalls and a nice mirror. I bought myself a pair of form-fitting levis — and a really thick ring.

Summer came and I lucked out. I stopped pumping (not that I minded it; I was always "up" when I was pumping) and got a job on a graveyard crew, transferring caskets and tombs. They were putting this new shopping center in where there was a cemetery so they had to dig up all the stuff and move it over to another lot. You had to live in quarantine a week before and two weeks after the seven-week job and, during it, live in a barracks with the other guys on the crew. I'd never lived with anybody before, but the pay was incredible — two hundred dollars a week, clear, so I took the job and just sent the checks straight into the bank. And in August, when I got unquarantined and was on my own again, I had sixteen hundred bucks to spend on my frame. I got a new engine, a rebuilt Chevy engine, some Koni shocks, and a new carburetor manifold. I had a little money left over. So I bought three cashmere turtlenecks for myself.

I guess having money, being able to be so good to my frame, gave me a taste for something. Anyway, come fall, I had this decision. The graveyard company I worked for traveled all over the state moving cemeteries. It was kind of morbid work, and they didn't get really top-notch people all the time, and the foreman, who was really pleased with my digging, called me up about a week before I was supposed to go back to school into my junior year, and he asked if I could dig permanently. I said I had to go to school. He said I didn't now that I was sixteen, and he said that he would give me a twenty-five buck raise, $225 a week, if I would stay on. I told him I'd think it over, got in my frame, went for a turn in her, looked at the slashed upholstery and the paint chips all over the

hood, looked at how dark and hard my arms were from the summer's digging and the Coppertone, drove right home, called him
back and said I'd take it, take the job. He really was happy; he
even laughed. My parents were a different story though. They
were ticked. They kicked me out.

So I got a room, a place in an old house with a high covered
bed, a chest of drawers and a huge mirror, and that cut out some
from my checks. Still, there was plenty left for the frame. I have
to tell you that I really missed her during the next ten weeks (more
than the first time; and we were only two towns away), but when
it was over, I rushed back and bought her new chrome (*all over*),
a new midnight-blue paint job and some CanAm bucket seats with
hand-laminated fiberglass, upholstered in forty-two-ounce Naugahyde. I got the forty-two-ounce Naugahyde for the *back* seat too,
and it looked beautiful. We drove around a lot. We went to drive-
in restaurants (I lived on double-cheeseburgers), drive-in laundries,
to the auto-window at the bank. And at night I went to movies,
drive-ins. And all the time my frame was working better and
better — more smoothly. It was great to be able to *do* that, make
that happen, help. Then I went off to another grave job.

Some of the guys on the crew were bothered by the smell, but
not me. To me it was like the smell of Naugahyde or the smell
inside my frame the first day when I sat in her in the snow and
imagined, with the gasoline soaked in my sneakers, that I was an
artist. So I could never understand the complaints. I didn't talk
to the other guys much anyway. They were mostly older and had
begun to look like their work. They had no brains. At night, in
the barracks, I used to stay pretty much by myself, sketching
fenders and gear sticks on a small pad of paper, sometimes a bird
beak or a wing. It was after New Year's when I finished my third
cemetery, and this time, when I went back, I bought an Autocross
Sound System, *everything*, even T.V. and tapes. I got myself eight
pair of shoes.

There were other things I wanted for my frame. But because
it was January and winter the company laid off for about three

months until the ground got soft again, and I was stuck with paying rent, buying all my own meals, and not having any money coming in until maybe April. So I had to conserve.

And that's the way it went. Nine months of digging, hurrying home, buying things for the frame, *fantastic* things — I'll tell you about them in just a minute — then three months off, just getting by, being *with* her all the time but having to hold back. Until I turned twenty-one.

By my twenty-first birthday, she had *everything*: Semperit tires, a Hewland gearbox, Aeroquip/A.M. hoses and fittings, tire pyrometers, beautiful rod ends, Gurney-Eagle cylinder heads, magnesium rocker covers, a rocker-arm shift assembly, beautiful cylinder head studs, two Carello quartz iodine lamps (for fog), a unison carb synchronizer, a Judson Electron magneto, a SCCA scattershield.

And that's not all! She had a capacitive discharge ignition system, disc brake pads, polyurethane-impregnated ballistics nylon fuel cells, a roller tappet cam, four six-inch seventy-two-spoke wire wheels, a seat belt, stabilizer, Sebring mirrors, a fiberglass "sleek-back" top (silver). *All* now with a 377 Cid Gurney Westlake rebuilt Ford engine. Over $8,000 worth of stuff on a $150 frame. She was a piece!

I felt I should do something, celebrate, show her off, take advantage of my age, my freedom, compare my frame to the rest of America. So I bought myself a black leather jumpsuit (I'm small; it made me look like a bullet) and started driving. I drove west, staying mostly on the turnpikes just to see what kind of time I could make. I hit big motels every night, places with pools and bars, and I ate nothing but steaks and drank straight vermouth. People used to come up and just touch my frame. I could pull my motel curtains apart just slightly from inside and watch. They were amazed. They had never seen a frame like that before. Everything was just perfect, just beautiful — until Nebraska.

It had started to snow. It was a Thursday and I was driving Nebraska and it had started to snow about ten-thirty in the morning. I didn't think much about it. The heater was perfect; I'd driven snow before. But then it started really coming down, thick, so thick the flakes hardly separated. And then the wipers stuck. I got out and cleaned them off, but in a minute they'd just stick again, worse. They were good wipers! They were GlideArt wipers! And I couldn't see.

It was impossible. So I pulled over. Snow stops — I knew that; snow stops. So I just kept the engine on, for heat, and waited. I tried the T.V., but the reception was nothing, so I turned it off and listened to the radio instead. It was better. I took out my pad of paper and had begun drawing spoked wheels, trying to see how many spokes (they began somehow to look like feathers) I could get on a wheel, when I heard kind of a "thud."

I listened. I turned off the radio. I couldn't hear much else. I thought maybe some clump of snow had fallen from a telephone wire overhead or something, so I went back to sketching spokes. But it came again, the "thud": dull, muffled.

I got out, looked around, looked up overhead. I couldn't see anything, nothing that would make a sound like that. So I got back in and in a minute it was there again, repeated.

This time I really inspected, walked around the car, until I saw. The gazelle, the silver gazelle I had in front of the engine hood had been torn off. And all the hubcaps were gone. And all the spokes off the right front wheel. I just stood there, the snow piling up on my hair and on the lids of my eyes, and it was like some doctor had just told me I had cancer and had only three more weeks to live. I couldn't understand anything.

Nothing was anywhere. I looked, and nothing was anywhere — except snow. It was impossible that those things were gone. The *snow* couldn't have torn them off.

I was getting cold. So I went back inside.

The snow was melting down over my face in little trails when it happened again. I jumped outside, looked everywhere, just stood and spun and looked around. No one. Nothing. Still — one of the Carello quartz iodine lamps on the front was gone. And my side

Sebring mirror.

I was scared. Things were going.

I went inside. It happened again. And then again. I was numb; I was afraid to step outside to see what was gone this time. It happened again. I was going to die; I knew it. Something I didn't understand was happening and I was going to die. Through the snow, through the windshields, I saw a mittened hand appear and rip the aerial off the hood. I got angry. I jumped outside and *this* time saw them: two guys in white parkas and ski masks on skis disappearing into the blur with my aerial and fistfuls of spokes. *Now*, I thought; now it's different!

I took a road-flare — just to use as some kind of spear — from the trunk and waited. There was no sound. Nothing had weight, not even the snow — except that it fell. Before I could see them again, they were there, knocking the flare away with one ski pole, pinning me to the car with two others. I could feel the points, silver and thick: one on my heart and the other on my groin, ready to puncture me. I yelled at them: *"Leave my frame alone!"* but off came the second Carello lamp just the same; off came my tire pyrometers. And they skied off.

I got angrier. I'd pumped gas *four* months for that frame. I'd carried *bones*. It had eight thousand bucks' worth of *stuff* on it, and I'd bleed or freeze to death before they'd get it.

I could make a flamethrower. I could burn them down. I had more flares in the trunk.

But the matches wouldn't light, and the wheel of my lighter kept making only small-sparked half circles. My thumb started to turn gray. I was afraid to try lighting anything inside the car, afraid the whole frame might explode. Then, when I went around toward the front of the car for more shielding, I saw that half the chrome and grillwork were gone.

I made a bomb. I emptied all the flare powder (eight flares) into a thermos bottle I had, then worked a hole through the rubber stopper with a corkscrew and fit a shoelace through it for a fuse. I had a pretty strong arm from my graveyard experience and I figured I could lob the bomb between the skiers the next time they made off and get them both. I sat inside, the cigarette lighter pushed in ready for the fuse, waiting.

The hood rose up. I don't know how they did it, because the hood lock was inside; still, I pulled the cigarette lighter out and lit the fuse. There were tearing and cracking sounds under the hood. With the bomb in my right hand, I began to push down very slowly on the driver's doorhandle. The handle slipped gradually about an inch, then held. I checked the button, but it was up. Still the lock held. Somehow they'd jammed it! I tried the other side, but it was the same. Then as I shifted, leaned back to my own side, I saw the fuse in the thermos which I was now holding between my legs, slipping down out of sight.

I pinched at it, got the end (it burned my fingers) just before it slipped out of reach. I couldn't tell, though, whether I had put it out or not. I couldn't see.

I tried the windows, but they were all frozen shut. I beat on them, and yelled. I kicked, but they wouldn't break; they stayed tight. And all the time there was tearing and pulling going on under the hood — I could hear it — parts, all my things being stripped off and taken. I knew I'd be blown up inside my frame; I knew I'd die; I was positive of it. I buried the thermos-bomb under the back seat, but I knew it wouldn't help much; it was just above the fuel line, and if the first blast didn't get me, I knew the second one would. And all the time things were being taken. I could hear them working now, under the car.

I screamed. I don't know what I screamed but I screamed. I went crazy. I could see myself from outside through the snow, the way *they* must have seen me: black leather jumpsuit, mouth opening and shutting, fingers clawing at the scattershield, no sound, no sense, a silent-rattling bullet. I was falling away.

I felt the front right corner drop. Then the back right. Then the other two corners. They had the wheels! What would they want next?

My door opened suddenly and I shot out of it and ran, ran as fast as I could just *away*, because I was sure my frame would explode. I kept waiting for it as I floundered through the snow, wondering if it could possibly be louder than the blood beating inside my head, but it never came, nothing louder, nothing more splitting-apart than myself. I slowed down. I stopped.

Something had frozen. My hearing had stopped. I couldn't smell or taste anything. And the snow! — I couldn't tell now whether it fell or rose; because it struck against both my forehead and my chin and then seemed to stand still altogether, tight, frozen in the air. I had no idea where my frame was. I thought probably I was dead.

I thought of birds. I stood there thinking of birds. I had a Clark bar in my coat pocket and I unwrapped it and broke it up and threw it out into what seemed like space — all the while thinking of birds, imagining them there in the space all around. The crumbs went. They *became* the snow and the space warmed. I had a sudden sense of where my frame was and I moved off in that direction, feeling more and more the possibility that I had not died at all.

And it was there — mostly buried, the frame, but I could tell that what I had invested, *all* of it, was gone, the "sleekback" top — *everything*. I could see *through* it, like a skeleton, like a tree without birds in winter, like a sketch penciled there in the air — the snow blowing through it. But somehow I didn't mind. It was the way it had begun; it was the way it ended. I had said all along that it was really the frame that I loved and I was ready now to stick by that and let it rest. Rust even. Do whatever frames do when they're left to themselves. It had been an experience.

I was nearly unconscious. A state highway plow found me inside my frame in the snow, my teeth frozen together, and took me to a clinic in Colon, the nearest town. It took me six weeks to recover, ups and downs but more ups. I work there now, in Colon in an electrical shop. I wire. I have a little room above Sawyer's Cafe, and I come home after work each night and I paint bones. Anatomy. Tibias, clavicles, femurs, thousands of ribs. It's a need.

I can't explain it. Someday, if I get good enough, I'd like to put my wiring and my painting together, perhaps for the little wildlife museum they have under the library, maybe build hummingbirds.

I walk to work.

Sometimes on weekends when it's warm, I drive my frame (I salvaged it) six miles out of town to a small lake there and swim — actually float. It feels nice driving alone. Because the breeze comes in through where the door and chrome and sleek-back top and shields used to be and feels cool.

Hunt

They were sitting in bed. New Hampshire farmers were preparing snowplows in barns and garages all down the highway and across the hills. The thermometer was stuck at zero. And it seemed unusually dark. Hunt told Leah that he thought he could almost hear the ice freezing on the lake outside, hardening with rigid snaps. Leah said that what he heard was the start of deer season. Then some time near dawn, Hunt told her. Leah shook. He tried to hold her. She fought him. Fought and then got up to pack.

"I'm going to take the children," she said.

"Where?"

"To tell your parents."

"It's still dark."

"I don't care."

"*I* do."

"You've made *your* choice."

But Hunt held Leah back until after breakfast. Snow had started. The sky looked like soft, faded stone. They put one bag and the children in the back of the wagon and set off for Boston to tell his parents about divorce. Every fourth car heading north, passing or passed by them, was racked and spread with a dead deer. "Isn't it awful!" one of the children said, as they passed a camper laden with two. In the rearview mirror, Hunt could see blood running down over the camper's windshield.

"I think my head is snapping," Leah said, almost trembling the seatbelt out of its lock.

"You'll be all right," Hunt said.

"That's what you think."

Saturday night, through what Hunt felt was a constant shaking of his upper bones, it was told. His parents listened, wept. They asked him questions. Leah listened. She said she felt she had a gun held at her head. Hunt said that he didn't want to go into it, string out histories, but there were reasons. He said he had been self-destructive and didn't want to be any more. Leah bit a nail until the cuticle bled. Afterwards, around ten o'clock, they all had drinks and built a fire. Hunt's mother noticed ants carrying other ants and crumbs of blue cheese across the hearth. She got a can and sprayed: "Everybody stand back," she said. "Cover your drinks." For a half-hour, before they all went to bed, they sat and watched the ants die and talked about the roots and meanings of "formication."

"Ants are actually theological," Hunt's father, a professor at both Harvard and MIT, said.

In the night Hunt and Leah laughed about the possibilities of ants in their navels, under their arms. They made good love in the morning and then showered.

"Get out of my bathroom, you bastard." Leah pushed him and laughed.

"O.K., lady," Hunt said. And all day Sunday, even driving back to New Hampshire, into snow, against the dark oncoming shapes of shot deer, they kept the good feeling.

But Leah couldn't sleep. She kept getting up, going to the window, staring out into the new bruise-colored snow, clutching her belly through her robe, walking down the hall to the bathroom, flushing something, walking back, standing at the window, re-entering only briefly the bed, moving back again to the window.

"Are you all right?" Hunt asked her.

"No."

"Come back to bed."

"No."

"Please."

"No."

"Take a Librium."

"Why?"

"You'll feel better."

"I don't know that I want to."

And so Hunt sat up most of the night, watching her in the dark, listening to her cry. It was a kind of crying he had never heard from Leah before: far away and darkly guttural. She sounded shot. She sounded as if there were something foreign lodged in her causing a rubbing, abrading pain. He got up out of the shadowed bed and tried to hold her.

"No," she said.

"Why?"

She stared down from their bedroom at the open entrymouths of their garage.

"Why won't you just let me take you back to bed?"

She just shook her head.

Leah cried while making breakfast for the children before school. Hunt watched then held her.

"Isn't Mommy feeling well?" one of the children asked.

"She'll be all right," Hunt said. "Look for animal tracks in the snow."

The children looked out of the windows. The sun was out, brokenly. One of them saw a plow moving slowly along the highway just across the lake. "Jays are frightening all the other birds away!" the other said. Leah cried harder, bore against Hunt's shoulder. Hunt could feel her small fists beating against his back. Was it him or herself that she was beating? Hunt wondered. And what would she do if she had a knife? He had the vague dark sense of pins at his shoulder caves.

Hunt and the children ate. Leah stood at the sink, refusing to turn off the water, staring at the jays.

"The radio said that last year, in the state, they shot over six thousand deer," she remarked. "That's a lot. That's an awful lot."

"People are butchers," Hunt said. Then he regretted it.

"People are," she said. "Yes, butchers."

"O.K.," he said.

"O.K. — what?" She turned to him.

He held one hand up, open. "Just O.K."

He walked the children to the bus, came back. Leah was at
another window, looking out, this time at the lake.

"Do you want to talk?" Hunt asked.

"When do you plan to leave?"

"We'll work it out."

"No."

"What do you mean, 'no'?"

"I mean, I'm not working anything out. Not any more. Not
now."

"Why?"

"Because you've got to *want* to work things out."

"You do. You will. It's just ..."

"No. No, that's the point bright-as-you-are you don't get. No.
No, I don't."

"Look ..."

"Hunt? Do you think any of those six thousand depopulated
deer drowned? Walked out on ice like that, fell through and just
drowned? Do you think any of them are at the bottom of this lake?"

"Leah, cut it!"

"Why? You've thought about death for fourteen years, haven't
you? Didn't you tell me that?

"Yes. But I also thought about life."

"Yes. But you see, you're whole now. Going to be whole.
You've made decisions. You're pursuing *balance*."

He couldn't paint. He tried working on a large oil street scene
from his past: lower Washington Street, Boston; but it wouldn't
shape or color. So he smoked. He smoked three cigarettes in his
studio, one fast after the other, and looked out. He watched the
snow. He watched wire-like branches and pines. He thought about
his uncle in New York who was a Jew. He thought about different

tones of white. He thought he could hear gunshots around the lake.

When he went to get more coffee, Leah was not around. He checked the downstairs bathroom. He checked upstairs. He went out to the garage, and the car was there, Leah's keycase dangling from the ignition key in the lock. She had thought about leaving them, going somewhere. Where? Hunt wondered where she would go. To his parents again? To see them? Why? Driving? Just driving? Snowy roads scared her: driving through snow? *Leah . . .*

"Leah . . . ?" Hunt called into the landscape. "Leah!"

He went inside, called her throughout the house. He checked the closets. He checked the medicine cabinets, not sure for what: bottles emptied of pills? He checked the furnace room, checked his studio lofts. There was nothing but the smells of oil and cold fishing gear.

Outside the kitchen door, Hunt found tracks. They led through the snow, circling, wandering past the back of the house, around the edge of the lake.

"Leah!" he called again. But it was like yelling out into foam.

He followed the tracks. The steps were short, absent-minded. They were all very close together, overlapping in some spots. Hunt wondered how long she'd been gone. How long had he tried to paint Washington Street? How many cigarettes had he smoked? How long had he thought about tones of white, about his uncle in New York who was a Jew? There was wind, low wind moving around the trunks of trees. The snow moved and salted over itself, lightly. And the water, skimmed in places with ice, looked very black. At one point Leah's tracks moved toward it, toward the edge. Hunt thought it possible that he would find her in it, standing in it up to her chest, looking out through some window of the just past night and morning that she had brought with her.

And the birds. Dark scissor-like birds. Around branches and within spaces to the side. They made sounds. They were gossipy, old, thin, black crone birds, filled with rumors, shuttling, now visible, now out of sight. Hunt thought of Brueghel landscapes, bird traps set up in gray, grainy snow. He stopped. He saw snow:

lines of it drawn on the tops of branches, speckled on the wind side of dark-umber trunks, caught in crotches. It was still November, but there were no signs of fall left. Total winter! Not a dangling stiff leaf. Even a negative of death, Hunt thought: dark bones, dark skeletons against a cold lifeless white. Hunt expected suddenly to see Brueghel's lean, unleashed dogs there too, or a living skeleton, perhaps a fleshless horse. Was Brueghel agnostic? Hunt tried to think. Did he believe? He felt a wind; he moved on, followed.

Then suddenly there was blood. In the snow in front of him, on the path, there was snow-granulated blood, small craters red and white, where it had dropped. Hunt screamed "Leah!" But there was nothing. So he ran.

He could hear the wind. He could hear water sucking against rocks to his right. And the blood was a trail now. It was in the snow, dropping almost regularly. Hunt could feel his own blood beating against the sides of his head as he ran.

The doe lay shadowy in the lake-edge path. Somebody had shot her in the side. She was dying but not yet dead. She lay there, as Hunt came upon her, bleeding into the snow. He slowed, then stopped. He stood and looked at her. He saw her fallen there in the white, legs drawn up. He felt that she watched him . . . with *something*; Hunt thought, with *something*, because her eyes were unseeing. Still she watched. She hoped, it seemed. Hoped? For what? Hunt imagined it was to trust him. Hunt imagined it was hope that he would not draw a gun and put another hole in her side. Hunt imagined that it was that he would not take a knife and move to her and open her belly up and remove her heart. So that he could suck on it. So that he could hurl it off into the branch tops for the dark birds.

Hunt drew a breath. *Hoped.* Then he drew several more. He and the deer held each other briefly with a mutual sight. Then Hunt moved to her. He knelt down. Hunt laid his head on her wound and tried to hear the tide of it — in and out. Or perhaps he was listening only to the lake. She seemed still warm. The skin was stiff but still living. She didn't move. She lay quiet. She made no attempt to escape him or to retreat. Maybe it was only that even that was gone — that will, that initiative. And Hunt wept. *Goddamn Brueghel*, he thought; *goddamn his truth.* Then suddenly her side seemed to explode. She convulsed. Her breath sparked from her nose. Her ribs, her entire rib cage and wound clenched. A moment later, she was quiet, living, still, accepting Hunt or whatever came.

He did not try to touch or move the doe. He left her there and backed slightly away. Her head turned slowly, slowly, watching him. Her eyes, it seemed — or perhaps it was simply the light — her eyes had dissolved almost completely now into their glass. If there was sight, it was buried. If there was vision, it was so small that he would have to approach her again, close, *close* to find out. And he didn't want to do that.

He found Leah a half-mile further down the lake-border path. She was simply standing in the white. She had no coat on, no gloves, no hat. Her skin was loose on her face. And without hue. Hunt could not see any texture there, or pores.

Leah was staring out over the lake. It was hard to say at what, at what object or point. She only stared. Her breath moved in and out of her like thin film. Hunt touched her.

"Leah . . ."

She showed no recognition of him. Her mouth was slack. Almost like the deer's her eyes seemed nearly vanished inside her head. Hunt turned her around. He led her back along the path. Her feet followed his carrying of her upper body and lent support. Branches bent in the way, but Hunt took them with his head for both of them. It was hard to think. There was a network of branches and connections; causes, effects; positions, aftermaths — penciled lightly somewhere within him, between brain and eye. Hunt did not want to, but could dimly see the pattern, like a web of veins seen only at times under pale, vulnerable, translucent skin.

Hunt moved Leah on.

He circled her out through the woods, around the deer, so that she would not see. Leah made no sound and gave no sign that she retained any present awareness of snow, rocks, branches, water, birds, clouds, of the world. Hunt brought her back. He could smell the fireplace smoke. He brought her in and sat her down. He took off her wet shoes and socks, put a pair of his own heavy socks on her feet. He built up the fire, pulled a couch over in front of it, laid her down, covered her up with her quilt.

But she didn't sleep. She just lay there with her eyes open until night, when the children were both upstairs, and then she asked him if there had been any *pleasant* times. Hunt said *yes; of course.* He told her of them. He spoke in images: birds, water, light, branch patterns, shore, dogs, a farm. He used the colors buff, burnt sienna, white.

"Thank you," Leah said. "Thank you." And they both slept.

But before Hunt slept, he thought once again of Brueghel, his *Hunters in the Snow*, his *Triumph of Death*. And he wondered.

Cordials

It wasn't until the waitress brought her Benedictine and she felt her first contraction that Lynn even thought of herself as being pregnant. She was thin anatomically and had managed to conceal her condition for well over seven months with a regimen of boiled turnips and cold consommé — and the reminder was badly timed to say the least. She had wanted to sleep with David Marker from the time she and Jack had spent a Saturday with the Markers sailfishing three months ago out at Wildwood, but there'd been interference at just about every point. She had called him; he had called her; they had met one afternoon at her apartment only to find her son Adam home from Hotchkiss as a surprise. Fall in New York is a difficult time to have an affair: everything starting up, schedules overcrowded again; so this evening was to have been an island for both of them.

"Something the matter?" David asked her.

She smiled. "No."

"You winced."

"Just anxious, I guess."

"As am I."

She rubbed the knuckles of his hand, climbing each ridge, kneading the loose skin in the depressions with her forefinger and thumb.

"Do you want to leave now?" he asked.

"Let's finish our drinks," she said, glancing at her watch, wondering when the next contraction would come. It came seven minutes later, in the midst of their quiet talk. She drained her glass: "All through," she said.

David smiled, breathed in his Drambuie and drained it. "Let's go," he said.

"Where are we . . . ?"

He helped her on with her coat. "A friend lent me his studio."

"Where?"

"Rowayton."

"That's an hour."

"Fifty minutes. And it's a nice Indian summer day. We'll drive with the windows down. Sea smell's an aphrodisiac."

"I don't need an aphrodisiac." Her voice was surprisingly soft and quiet.

David nodded to the maitre de, and pushed the door open; she went out. "It's a great place — this place — this studio."

Lynn breathed the late September West Fifty-second Street smells, and felt another contraction coming on.

When they cloverleafed onto the Merritt Parkway, the tugs were coming regularly, just under five minutes apart. Both the front windows were down. David had the heater on; her coat was beside her on the seat. She had her face against his neck, her jaw pressed there. She'd worn no bra — she didn't really need one — and he was moving the tips of his right middle fingers over the nipple, under her burgundy knit.

"You're perspiring," he said, trying to sound playful.

"Yes. It's the heater. The blower's going right up my dress." She knew, in fact, that her breasts were lactating. "Rowayton?"

"There are fourteen-foot ceilings," David traced her neck. "And a fireplace."

"Had you planned on using the fireplace?"

"For a fire, sure; not for us."

"I don't know if I can wait." Lynn felt her body tightening again, watched the speedometer climb from seventy to eighty-five.

"You'll love it," David said to her; "it's on the shore. You can hear the ocean. Waves. It's a great rhythm. Great keeping time to. Natural. Nothing rushed." He let his hand slide slowly down to her leg. She picked it up, kissed it. She looked at her watch: three minutes and twenty seconds; she picked up and kissed his hand again when she felt the next contraction; three minutes and fifteen.

"How long until we get there?" she asked him.

"Twenty — twenty-five minutes." He played with her nipple again. She held her breath. "You're really remarkable," he told her. "I've been clawing New York's concrete for three months."

"Me too," she said, "I've been having the most amazing fantasies."

"I'm not very good at waiting," David told her, then smiled.

"Nor am I." She thought about it; it was true. "I wait for very few things."

"Waiting fantasies are strange." He began to slide his hand down to her abdomen. "They make you feel almost adolescent." She picked up his hand again, kissed it, checked her watch. "Your heart's jumping."

"There's a motel in Mamaroneck," she said.

"One quarter-hour, *max*," he told her. The pains were coming every two minutes plus.

When they pulled in beside the studio and cut their lights, Lynn's spasms were only a minute, or slightly more, apart. Like a schoolboy, David started to undress her in the car; she put two hands against his chest: "Let's go inside."

He smiled, "O.K.," then kissed her eyes, let himself out, and walked around to her door. She could smell the sea, as he'd predicted, and it smelled as though her own body had become huge, grown unlit and infinite, and moved outside to become anatomy in the night around her. She became her own child briefly — undelivered though dependent and scared. She thought of a time when she was fourteen, parking out near Coney Island with a boy named Arnold, the "Tennessee Waltz" on the car radio, how her whole mouth had trembled, how her thigh muscles had gone slack. She heard the door button click, felt the sea wind against her hair, smelled the blown redolence of herself.

Lynn didn't like being aggressive. She had always hated the role; it ruined everything. But she pulled David into the room, and when he wanted to get a fire going, she said *no*.

"Why not?"

"Please."

"Lynn, that's the whole . . ."

"Afterward!"

"I may want to sleep."

"Please!"

"O.K."

She pulled him to the bed.

She had continually fantasized David's undressing her, for three months had lived it in her mind: its being gentle, slow; kisses, where he placed them, breast, belly, hip; when they came. And so against her better judgment she let him, let it work out, let the imagining come true. True: she stood there, in the dark, arching, moving, turning slightly for him on the balls of her feet. And David carried it off: it was worth the concealment, worth the pain. The hands played, the kisses came on time, in form. She felt the zipper on her dress move down, slipped her arms out, felt the dress fall around her hips. She felt her water break. "David," she said, and pulled him to her.

She dug at him, made his shoulder bleed, bit his face. It helped to get the pain out. He was trembling, "Jesus! Jesus-God! Jesus, Lynn," he said. "God, come on! Off our feet! Off our feet! Talk about adolescents! God!"

"Then get undressed," she told him.

"You!"

"David . . ."

"Do it. You — "

His jacket was already off. His neck was moving on its base; his breath was heavy and wet. "Christ, you're incredible! You're incredible!" he said.

She couldn't help it. They were somewhere between twenty and thirty seconds apart now, and the pain and pressure were too much. She grabbed the collar of his shirt and tore, ripped it down, spread it, snapping all the buttons in a line. They landed, light as crickets, on the rug. "Fantastic!" David was moaning. "Oh, fantastic! Wow!" She yanked his belt. "Oh, God!" She felt it uncinch. She broke the button above the fly and heard the zipper whine. She pulled the pants past his knees.

"O.K.," she managed, her voice strained and tight, "You do the rest."

"No. Please." He was rocking. "You. The shoes!"

"David . . ."

"O.K., I'm sorry." He stepped out of things. "I'm sorry." He let other things drop. She saw his shape sit on the bed's edge, pull his shoes off. She didn't know how she was going to make it as she removed her panties and walked toward him.

He pulled the bedspread down. She found a wastebasket and slid it beside the bed. She moved against him, kept his hands on her back, pressing her whole anatomy hard, violently down, against, trying to create enough pressure to displace some of the pain. She screamed. She dug in. She fought against him with her fists and knees. He kept bellowing sounds to match hers, saying things like: *God* — he thought his fantasies were pretty advanced, but — *Jesus* — he realized now that they were — *Christ* — naive. But as they tore and fought against each other, Lynn felt herself giving way and knew that what she'd hoped for was impossible. She could not last. She could not hold out.

She slid down his body slowly, marking it with her teeth, clearing herself as she could. When the baby came, it came easily and she was able crudely to slice the cord, get everything in the wastebasket, and cover it with the bedspread without really losing much of the rhythm of the foreplay. She submitted to David pulling at her, at her shoulders, slid back up along him, joining, both of them, three minutes later, coming almost together under the bloodsoak of sheets.

David lay with his head off the far edge of the bed, making sounds. Lynn played one hand over his ribs, blew breath gently against his sweat. She could smell herself — herself, the ocean, and her own birth, but could not keep them apart. She thought she heard a steamer, way out in Long Island Sound. Shortly afterward, while David showered, she took the basket out to the small pier of the studio front and emptied it into the sea. Standing there, she tasted herself again, her own fetality, felt the darkness — warm, salty, moist, in membranes layered out and out around her. The moon seemed a strange opening in space, a place she might ultimately go. She ached, but could not feel her body. It was an abstract ache, one in air.

Inside, they came together one more time: much quicker, less violent, more studied, more synchronized. David did not shower. Instead, he dressed himself hurriedly and lit a long cigar.

"Did I hurt you?" he asked. "I'm always afraid . . ."

"No," Lynn reassured him from the bathroom. She stopped herself with toilet paper, pulled on her panties, and dropped her dress over her head. "No." Somehow it was true.

"Hey — you start?"

"What?"

"Your period start?"

"Yes."

In the car, on the way back to Manhattan, they talked enthusiastically about St. Croix.

Her husband, Jack, was sitting on the long couch in his blue bathrobe, going through trial briefs when she came in. There was a small snifter of crème de cacao on the coffee table to his right. They said hello. She kissed him on his forehead and hung up her coat.

"Where you been?"

"Theater."

"What'd you see?"

"*Long Day's Journey.*"

"How was it?"

"Fantastic." She straightened her hair.

"Great play." Jack wrote a sentence in the margin of his brief. "There's some Triple Sec there, if you want."

"Thanks."

"Picked it up on the way home."

She poured a cordial glass half full. The smell of orange reminded her of Christmas, kumquats from Florida fruit packages she had bitten into in lost distant Decembers as a child. She crossed the room. She stood in front of the window wall, looking out. The lights beyond, below, all the bunched thousands of them, looked like perforations. She stared at the reflected milk stains on her dress. Her reflection seemed to spread across the city light perforations in the night to surround her until, as she searched the distance, her reflection diffused and was gone.

"Did you find it?"

"Hmm?"

"Find the Triple Sec."

"Yes. Fine. Thanks."

"See the letter from Ad?"

"No. What's he say?"

"They beat Taft twenty-one to twenty. He pulled a ligament in his knee. He's been having whirlpools. Nothing serious. They took X-rays at Sharon Hospital. He's seeing Cynthia Kaufmann this weekend. Listen — do you want to?"

"Hmm?"

"You at all horny?"

She pressed the cordial glass against her lips. The fruity taste rose up, viscous, wet. "Maybe later," she said.

"Can't hear you."

She took the glass away, wet her lips. "Maybe later."

"Sure, O.K."

Her eyes watered. She experienced the only moment akin to incest she had ever felt. She considered Adam, her son, in the whirlpool. And her knee hurt.

Dealer

At twenty-six, Hatch had lost, or lost at, almost everything: a father, a mother, college, a wife, their baby, any job. And so, trying to break a streak, Hatch packed an airline bag and took off, hitchhiking, on what he hoped was the beginning of a change. Hatch traveled west. He went to Columbus and pumped gas. At Independence, he lifeguarded at a Best Western motel. In Cheyenne, he wore a white hat and turned steaks at the Sizzler Grill.

In early spring, Hatch moved on west again, taking Route 80 out of Salt Lake City toward a series of towns whose names all began with "w": Wendover, Wells, Winnemucca. In Wells, he saw that the road north toward Idaho led also to a town named Jackpot in Nevada, and he took that, riding with an Indian driving a lumber truck. Neither of them spoke. They rolled north. They passed a stretch of fences called the Winecup Ranch, and, ten miles later, at four in the morning, the Indian stopped the truck and nodded for Hatch to get out. Hatch swung the door open without protest and stepped down. He watched the truck pull out and fade north along the only paved road in the nightscape; he followed, walking in its wake.

Gradually light came. The winter sun started up low in the east and Hatch found himself walking past foothills strewn with volcanic rock. Hatch wondered when the rocks had been thrown up on the hills. He sensed that his life, somewhere near here, soon would be different. Three miles later, in the town of Contact, he caught a milk truck that took him straight to Jackpot.

"This it?" Hatch asked, gesturing at a pocket cluster of three casinos and several motels and gas stations. The driver nodded, and Hatch took the weight of the small airline bag in his hand and wandered off toward the first casino, a sign flashing even with the dawn, off and on, off and on: *Cactus Pete's.*

Hatch had never been in a casino before. He had heard about them, read about them, imagined what Las Vegas must be like. But the minute he stepped inside, he knew he was home.

Something about the way light fell, about the smell, about the music — almost like an all-night radio station. Something about the sound of coins, about machines ringing, about the tin under-music of silverware in the coffee shop, about the reflection of ceiling mirrors, about the way people moved and stalked, about the way men in white shirts waited behind tables in the pit, about the dark wood on the bar, about the rugs: something about *all* of that made him forget the wind outside, made him forget his wife, the child, and the long paralysis of his father. Hatch was home. He put a nickel in a slot machine, won himself a dollar, had a cup of coffee and left all the other nickels for the countergirl as a tip. "Thanks," she said.

"Who would you see about a job here?" Hatch asked.

"See the man? Over there? With the white silk shirt and the hand-tooled leather belt?"

"Yes," Hatch said.

"You see him," the girl said.

Within twenty minutes Hatch had a room in the help's wing and a job as a guard on the graveyard shift, watching the slot machines. The man, Randolph, took him twice through the routine.

"We'll try you out," he said. "If you can do it, you're on."

"I can do it," Hatch assured him.

"What's your name?"

"Hatch."

"Just Hatch?"

"Hatch."

Hatch loved the work. He would watch for people using devices on the slots: plugs, nickels soldered to wires that could retract them. Xeroxed bills on the Big Bertha dollar machine. Hatch had an instinct for gamblers.

On his breaks Hatch loved to study the dealers. He would

watch them shuffle, watch the cards fan out, see all the hits dealt, watch the dealer turn his own down card over, take his own hit if it were necessary, scoop the chips in with his cards. It was all an image of fingertips, flashing like bird wings over felt; like small flames, like absolutely clear water: magical, dexterous.

Hatch bought some old packs of cards: "These cards have been in actual play at Cactus Pete's," the package said; and Hatch practiced dealing cards in his small room. There was a long mirror in front of a walnut-veneer dresser, and Hatch would stand there dealing first one hand, then two, then finally all six, imagining players. He would watch in the mirror as the cards fell, watch his hands. He was proud of them.

On his first day off, he hitchhiked to Twin Falls and bought himself a large piece of green felt. He cut the felt and fixed it with masking tape to the dresser. He taped six card boxes to deal to, spacing them in a slight arc. He had his own playing table, and he loved it, and he'd deal — sometimes four hours at a stretch.

On his next day off, Hatch bought chips and practiced playing with them: scooping in, stacking, paying. He was amazed at how little he had to pay off; how often he won. He could draw six cards to a twenty or twenty-one nearly every time without a break. It was strange. It was miraculous how the cards fell. Hatch felt select, he felt anointed and ordained. Cards turned in his favor, against all probability. He practiced "burning" the top card, a swift liquid motion moving it to the bottom after the cut so that no one could see what it was. Each day, for at least an hour, he would just shuffle. Finally, he chose the casino's best dealer and asked him to watch Hatch deal.

"You think you're ready?" the dealer asked.

"Can't tell," Hatch said. "Just can't tell."

The dealer watched for almost an hour. "Phenomenal," he finally said. "Unbelievable! I'll talk to Randolph." Then he left.

That night on his shift, Randolph came up to Hatch and took him to an empty table. He instructed him, then had him deal. Hatch won thirteen out of fifteen hands. "You're a natural,"

Randolph said.

He had Hatch deal out all six boxes: "Deal right to left. Pay off left to right. Tap your tips. Slap once when you walk away; shows you're clean." Randolph watched Hatch's hands, the agility, the brisk presumption of his cards. In ten rounds, Hatch broke only once and, outside that once, never had to pay off more than two of six.

"I think I could do better with real players there," Hatch said. "I think I could cool people. Cool people off."

"Tomorrow night," Randolph said, "you start dealing."

Hatch was an instant legend. No one won. He moved quickly from graveyard to day to prime shift. There was always a constant turnover at his table, but, at busy times, it didn't matter; people spent their money fast and moved out, and others with new money came in. Hatch took it all. There was never any expression on his face. His hands moved. They were machines. He just dealt. He saw eyes, watched the eyes watching him, but he never saw faces.

His reputation spread. Players came from Elko at first, then Tahoe and Vegas. "Where's Hatch?" they'd ask the pit boss. "We've heard about this guy named Hatch." And then they'd buy five hundred or a thousand dollars in chips and play two, some-times·three hands at a time. And Hatch would go through them like a trout through rapids, his mind fastened somewhere in the light that caught the blade-like edges of the dealt cards. Once a man from Sarasota stayed a week, sending home every other day for money orders, playing only when Hatch was on duty. They found him hanging in his motel shower, choked by his money belt. When Hatch heard about it, he touched the various bones that made up his head, but he could not really be said to have thought anything about the man.

Hatch bought things. The management gave him frequent bonuses, and he began, very selectively, to acquire. He bought leather: leather shirts, leather vests, leather pants; soft leather, smooth leather; natural leather, dyed leather. He bought almost a hundred pairs of shoes and almost fifty belts. To walk into Hatch's room at Cactus Pete's was to walk into the presence of sweatless animals, a place of only cool and scentless hides. And Hatch bought himself a horse, a fine Appaloosa that he named Horse, but he rode him only in winter, in snow.

In the days between December and early March, Hatch would ride the animal out, ride him south. They would walk into the rock formations below Contact — the more snow in the air, the better — and Hatch would weave a trail among the boulders. He would think of his father, of the unmoving silence in any air ever between them. He would see birds in his mind, brightly colored birds, frozen, falling through unwinded air onto a place like sea-coast, shattering. He would see animals, stiff and still and stone, standing in place, cracking, falling in fragments on a frozen ground. Then he would go home and, in the night, dream of rocks. His life had changed. He was not a loser anymore. He could win. And he could have a woman when he wanted. And he would always insist that she do everything.

That's what had happened toward the end of his second February. He had ridden Horse out into the snow-covered rocks at Contact. It had been nearly fifteen below zero, and he had stayed almost four hours without any movement, imagining deer shattering and tanagers plummeting, a weighted mass of shale and crystals inside his mind. Then he rode Horse back, took a shower, dressed for work, went to his table, and dealt.

Shortly after eleven, a woman took a place at his table. She had a look of terrified beauty that bore back far into her eyes. Hatch selected her. He watched her change two hundred dollars into chips and proceed to lose deal after deal. He saw her watching his shoulders and his hands. She had on a long blue skirt and a low-cut top, and, in exposed risings, her breasts looked polished, veined like good marble. Hatch finished his deal, brushed his hands once to show them empty, and moved off to the bar. She met him there.

"You're very good," she said.

Hatch nodded.

"Buy me a drink?"

Hatch held his hand up. The bartender came. Hatch pointed at the bartender for the girl.

"I'll have a whiskey sour, please," she said.

The bartender moved off.

"I'll bet you're a very cruel man," she said, her voice even. "The way you deal. There's something very . . ."

"I just deal," Hatch told her.

"No, you don't." Something like a smile appeared on her lips. "No, you don't. No."

"There's your whiskey sour," Hatch said. "I'll be back in about twenty minutes — if you want to lose more money."

"You live here?" She held him a moment with the question. "Yes."

"In the motel?" she said.

"Yes."

"What number?"

"Twenty-one," Hatch said, and almost smiled.

Minutes after he arrived back at his room, she knocked and came in. She took his clothes off, then removed hers. She kissed him and drew him to the bed. She pressed him down and stroked him. She talked to him, talked him up: almost a set patter, he thought. Like the stickmen at the craps table: "Number's four. You're knocking on the door." "Eight; eight; no field this time, but next time looks great." "Two; craps; two; a seven will do." "Coming out! Coming out this time." Hatch finished fast. She was nowhere near. She got up, dressed, and left. Hatch listened to the wind a moment. He could almost see it, like stiff celluloid. He saw a gazelle, inside the camera of his brain, become arterial with cracks, then fall apart. Hatch dressed and went back.

He started dealing. There was a man from Puerto Rico who had heard about Hatch in Reno and was there to beat him. He started playing fifty dollars a hand and lost seven straight. "Keep those cards coming from the top," he said. Hatch took another five hundred quickly. The man wanted to have Hatch drop the house limit: "Who do I see?" he asked. Hatch pointed to Randolph. Later, the man was back, betting one, two, then five hundred a hand. Hatch kept even, the Puerto Rican never winning more than one hand in five.

Hatch noticed the woman he'd just had, standing with a man Hatch took to be her husband. They stood at the craps table. Hatch saw her whispering to the man. The man looked back over his shoulder at Hatch. He saw the woman whisper again. The man looked back and fixed him with a stare. "Blackjack!" he heard the Puerto Rican say, five hundred dollars in chips sitting in the box in front of his seat. Hatch paid him off. "Why don't you bet it all the next time? See if you can win two in a row?" Hatch asked him, filaments of anger curling in his chest. The man took the challenge. The two pushed at nineteen apiece, pushed again with twenty. Then the man doubled down with an eleven and drew a seven to Hatch's nineteen. Hatch took his money back. The man started screaming, cursing Hatch in Spanish. He scooped in the few chips he had left and moved away. Hatch calculated that in nineteen mintues he had taken in seven thousand dollars for the house.

The man taking the Puerto Rican's chair was the blue-skirted woman's husband. He was dark. His hair was black. His cheeks were somehow knuckled, clutched with multiples of bone. He looked at Hatch. Hatch looked at him and at the woman standing about two feet behind; he dealt and broke on a hand while the man was getting money out. "E-O-eleven!" somebody yelled from the craps table. Three jackpot bells went off in chain. Hatch scraped a piece of lint from the felt in front of him.

"Five hundred in twenty-fives. A hundred in fives," the man said.

Hatch took the six hundred-dollar bills and changed them. The man set a five-dollar chip in his box. Hatch dealt himself a blackjack, ace and ten, and scooped all bets in. He felt the left-hand corner of his mouth flicker up. The woman's husband set a twenty-five-dollar chip out in front of his box, then replaced his lost five with another. Hatch looked at the twenty-five. "Tip," the man said, and the mirrors around the pit seemed, to Hatch, to catch a brief light. Hatch nodded to the man, set the tip aside for himself, and dealt again.

Hatch had a four showing. He dealt his hits, turned over a king, hit himself with a deuce and then a four. The woman's husband had an eighteen. Once more Hatch took in the losses and once more he saw the twenty-five-dollar chip set aside for him. He took it, nodded, and drew a breath. He saw the woman smiling behind her husband. Once more the mirrors over his head flashed. He thought of Horse, wondered if it were cold where the animal had been fenced.

Hatch took the man's five dollars a third time. The mirrors blinked. The woman smiled. The cocktail waitress passed taking drink orders: "The house would like to buy you a drink."

"Bourbon," the man said, "rocks," and set another twenty-five dollars out in front of him for Hatch.

"What's that for?" Hatch said.

"Excuse me?" the man said.

"The twenty-five," Hatch said.

"Same as the others." The man smiled. He smiled at the other players sitting at the table watching him. "Tip."

"But you lost." Hatch could feel his right knee vibrating. He pressed his foot into the carpet beneath him.

"Win some, lose some," the man said and smiled.

Hatch drew a breath, twisted his mouth, set aside the chip. "Maybe," he muttered.

He dealt again, won again: twenty. "You can't beat this guy," someone next to the man leaned over to advise him.

"Lose some, win some," the man said again and smiled. He set another twenty-five out for Hatch. Hatch shook his head, took it, and dealt. The man took a card and broke. This time he set fifty ahead of him for Hatch.

"But you *lost*!" Hatch almost shouted. The man's wife had her hand over her mouth, maybe hiding a smile.

"Lose s . . ."

"But that's insane!"

". . . some, win some."

Hatch raised his deck as if to throw it. The pit mirrors flashed and photographed him. People gathered. Hatch dealt out the hand, finished the others. Randolph came over. "Any problem?" he asked.

"I'm fine." Hatch bit hard, teeth against teeth.

"Sure?" Randolph said.

"Sure," Hatch said, and dealt.

Hatch won again. This time the man pushed him a hundred. Hatch leaned forward. "Look," he said to the man, as quietly as he could, "they're going to think I've got something going with you. I mean, why . . . ?"

"But you do," the man said, and smiled.

Hatch felt as though small stones were striking his chest. Everything appeared to be hardening into gems: tables, light, glass. He stepped back. The others were waiting for him. They were watching. Hatch noticed a man in a wheelchair playing at the next table. All around him, Hatch heard chips. Some of his bones Hatch thought he could feel slipping into new positions in his head and chest, realigning. Then he smiled. "You play with all kinds of people in a place like this," he announced to the crowd, those watching him, waiting. "Some just regular people — most. Some crazy. This man," he said, pointing to the woman's husband, whose chips sat in a stack beside him, "I think he's crazy."

The man smiled. Behind him, his wife smiled as well. Some in the crowd, Hatch's audience, laughed. Then the man pushed eight twenty-five-dollar chips forward to Hatch. The watchers rumbled. Hatch took a breath, bit, felt his jaw tighten, and took the money. "Thanks," he said politely.

"Pleasure," said the man.

Hatch dealt. He beat all except the woman's husband. Hatch had a twenty; the man drew an eight to his thirteen. Hatch paid off the five, then paused.

"No tip this time?" he asked.

"Not when I win," the man said, smiling. "Cuts the profits." Several people laughed. The cocktail waitress brought the table's drinks. The man changed two thousand dollars more into twenty-fives, a hundred more into fives. Hatch felt small flashes climbing his spine.

Hatch dealt this time and won. The man passed him three hundred, and Hatch felt another flash of the mirrors; he felt a muscle pulling, left to right, across his brain. Again he dealt. He broke. Again no tip. Hatch broke a second hand. "Lose some, win some," the man said, keeping all twenty-fives to himself, hold-ing on tight, offering nothing. Then Hatch won: jack and queen for a twenty. The man smiled and passed Hatch five hundred dollars; Hatch threw the deck down and across the table. Watchers quieted. Others moved in. Randolph crossed the pit from the craps table: "What's going on?" he asked.

"Nothing," Hatch muttered, picking the cards precisely, one by one, from the felt.

"I don't get it," Randolph said.

Hatch looked at the black and red numbers coming up: four, seven, queen, six, nine, ace. "Nothing," he said. "I was dealing. I was trying to deal too fast, that's all. I was dealing — nothing." He held his breath.

"Take it easy," Randolph said, pressing a fist into a shoulder blade, smiling out at the table. "Easy." And then, off and across the pit. "Jan! Could we have more drinks at this table, please?"

Randolph moved away. The woman's husband passed Hatch another two hundred. Jennings, Hatch's relief dealer, tapped Hatch on the shoulder to take over. Hatch fanned the cards out on the felt with a stroke, brushed his hands, grabbed up his tips, dropping some, retrieving them, nodded to the players, and walked, moving fast, outside.

Snow blew over the empty highway and through the lights from the Casino across the street, the flakes smelling like wet stone. Hatch lifted his head and breathed hard. Snow flew in, flew in sharp into his nose and felt jagged against his face. In the dark he sensed his eyes and mouth: not hard, not boned, but crushed and soft. He started walking. Boulders seemed to be rising up, huge stones lifting against the snow, looking like moons in the low air. The air was filled with undiscovered rocks. Enormous things rose. Hatch was crying. He and his father were talking about catcher's mitts, the ball sailing back and forth between them; talking about catcher's mitts, talking about pockets, talking about breaking gloves in, talking about the best catchers in the leagues.

Hatch drove his hands into the sheered rock at the highway's edge: repeatedly, repeatedly.

It was hard, back again, to deal cards with bandaged hands. In the first half hour, Hatch won only two-thirds of his deals; by the end of the evening's shift, less than half. He had eighteen thousand dollars in tips from the man; but the man was beating him regularly now, over the evening taking about three thousand from the house.

"Thanks," he said to Hatch at four when Hatch went off. "Thanks," his wife said, standing behind him still and smiling.

Hatch looked at the man and started at the bones of his face. He thought of shoulders. Of necks. And of backs. He thought of a woman. Of an infant. An infant's feet. Of his mother's forehead, in the fluorescent light, in the kitchen late at night. Hatch nodded.

"Lose some, win some," the blue-skirted woman said.

"You're a good sport," her husband nodded in time.

"Hard as stone," the woman said.

"Tough as nails," said the man.

"Cold as ice," the woman said.

Hatch moved away.

Two weeks later, when anyone could beat him, after work one morning Hatch packed his airline bag with whatever clothes he could fit and left. He rode Horse down from Jackpot, down past Contact to the Winecup Ranch and left him, inside the fence, to be taken care of.

Peterson's Stones

Peterson first found the stones in late spring on an eastern bank of Lake Huron. The stones were flat, gray, and layered, very much like shale, and the first one was marked with a fernprint on its face. The second had the stamp of a fish's spine. Peterson had never touched fossils, only seen them beyond glass or in encyclopedias. It made him shake slightly to hold them. The wind blew in steadily from a hazed shoreless west. Peterson's hair fluttered. He held the stones, one in each hand. On the face of a third, unmistakably, was the scar of a New York City subway token.

Something had happened three years before to Peterson. He had killed his friend the Jesuit. They had been sailing out of York Harbor in Maine when the boat capsized with Peterson at the tiller. The wind had been a voice only, an oboe. They had been boys together: played hockey, read H. G. Wells, Poe, and Orwell. The Jesuit had worn a white windbreaker, and had laughed insanely when the water plumed suddenly up and he was gone. The last words that Peterson had heard him shout were: . . . *should have eaten!* Then the tide devoured him. Everyone else had said: "Undertow." But Peterson knew. His hands in the dark were always figured with small blood-like hieroglyphs.

So Peterson hardened, grew more spare. His mind focused down. He sold his furniture. He seldom spoke. His parents moved to St. Croix. He adored a woman but left her. He inherited a farmhouse where the hay smelled almost fruity after rain, but Peterson had all the plumbing replaced and sold it. After that he moved to New York and became involved with industrial diamonds.

Etched on the fourth stone was a Shell Oil Company credit card: #591 802 747; expiration date: 0774.

It was June. Peterson was in Ontario, Canada, on his way to see a mine in Montana. He was on the Bruce Peninsula and had driven all morning behind a hayrake through towns with names like Kinloss, Chesley, Ambleside, Listowel — names he had never heard before. Angus cattle grazed the fields but seemed unreal, like brooding anthracite forms. He saw redwings and mourning doves. He had never been in Canada before.

On the far outskirts of a town named Wiarton, a sign directed Peterson to: *Cape Croker.* He turned right. The asphalt dissolved to gravel, gravel to dirt; the road thinned. And Peterson thought: *Wild!* There were sheer granite cliffs, white, rising all around; pines; ponds; dense wildflowers — bluet, wild crocus, lupine, starberry — alive in coarse and feathery grass, in woods, in water, by water's edge. Butterflies populated the air. Beauty seemed unrestrained, without limit, as if it could claim, assume, overrun every track of road.

Peterson had no idea where he was. He stopped his car, removed his sunglasses, pressed his hands hard against his temples, closed his eyes, and drew a breath. He had always called his friend, the Jesuit, a Primitive. Why? He felt harebell and sweet william crowding.

Peterson drove. He found the tip of the cape, where the neutral air held no direct sun or insects. When he stepped out and first saw the lighthouse, he felt dizzy. Suddenly there was water again chopping high; wind; a tiller; his hand felt scarred. Images swept over him before he could label them: a baseball, its stitching; the loose sleeves of a windbreaker. But then the sea impressions mineralized; they grew hard and clear. He scanned the water, breathed in air, took some beer and cheese from a cooler in his trunk, and started walking along the shore. He saw fish jump. The wind smelled smoked, like dry-ember hickory coals, cut with clove. That was when Peterson began finding the stones.

The fifth stone carried on it the clear expansion ribbing of a watchband.

They were everywhere! A car key with GM printed on it. Coca Cola in cursive. A disc with "Harrah's Club/$25," centered. Clear impressions of razorblades, aluminum lid pulls, wedding rings, transistors, Lego toys, light filaments, golf balls, sprinkler heads. Peterson walked along the shore, cradling the best of the stones like tiny birds along his arm, then he returned and laid them out in careful rows on the bank.

Peterson's eyes went from one stone to another. He knelt quietly, reached out a hand, and felt the stone braille of objects. His throat drew tight. He heard the water coming in behind him. *He believed in nothing.* The thought came and went suddenly. His eyes seemed oversensitive to light. He looked around. There was no one there; there were no houses, even, that he could see; no cars, no smoke columns, no power lines. *Why had he left New England, gone to New York, turned to hard, broken jewels?* He laid his fingers on the stones again, touched and played with them. They made sounds like piano chords, chords as brief and as under-towed as certain offshore swells and waves: a crowded subway — gone; a wedding reception — gone; downtown Boston traffic — gone.

It swept through Peterson that with the grayish silt, with the water tables rising and falling, the baking sun, the dry air — annual, almost instant fossils could be, were in fact born. On this very shore! He thought about all the things lost or thrown into water: the ring, the ballpoint cartridge, the corkscrew, the . . . motel key, the single earring, the cross, . . . the capped tooth. He turned and scooped up some of the clay. It would work. He heard the chords again, lost sounds abandoned in the water. He turned and looked up at the white distant cliffs. There was something like calligraphy on them, etched, but he could not make it out. Peterson set the gathered stones carefully in the trunk of his car. He started off toward the cliffs.

The dirt roads were maze-like, sometimes dead-ended, some-times intercepting one another again and again. Peterson, as he drove, left no map in his mind, only watched the strangely figured

stone faces and drove toward them. From his trunk perhaps, linger-
ing like breath around his fossils, came the damp spirit-smell of
clay. He drove closer. He parked; he got out; he climbed near.

The first glyph that Peterson deciphered on the cliff chalk was
the grill of a 1969 Mercury Montego.

Peterson, set in motion by some incalculable force, followed
the cliff base. Stone pictures were above him everywhere, petro-
glyphs — the tail section of a Boeing 747. Then came the clear
face of a cigarette machine; ten feet of chain link fence; an air-
conditioner duct; the cross section of a snowblower. He walked
more than a mile, a mile and a half, stopped, shook his head, and
walked back again, memorizing: locker doors, urinals, intestinal
refrigerator coils; a gasoline pump, a switchboard, a bridge truss.
   Peterson touched the aerial of his car. He shook. He could
taste the attic in his grandmother's house, smell an ancestry there
of vests and innertubes and sails. He heard a sound — *scrape/
whoosh* — like the early morning shoveling of snow: *memories.*
He touched in his mind the dormers of the room where he and the
Jesuit, boys, had sat, hours, talking about the haunting of their
house, had played darts, monopoly. Peterson pressed his eyes. He
heard women's voices saying to him: "Peterson — who are you?"
And he could sense his head against small pillows in enormous
planes. And he could feel how terribly cold his fingers felt crooked
around sliding doors of ice machines in motels. What was going on?
   He got in his car and drove away, turning variously in the
puzzle of roads. He came to a dead end, turned, and drove out.
The road graduated into gravel, became a "T." Peterson went
right, took another quick left. The road turned back to dirt. There
were no other branches or side roads. Once again, flowers began
to overgrow. He could smell the fossils. Peterson turned his car
radio up. He spun the dial for news. He could find only banjo and
flute music. What looked like cattails began cropping into the road.
Peterson turned the radio off, hollered: "Out!" Redwing black-

birds dove in front of him. Dust rose up. He could not see water anywhere. There was no indication of either cape or light. There was just an old Indian in the road.

Peterson honked. The old Indian wouldn't move. Peterson honked again. Cabbage moths blew like ashes into the unsettled air. Peterson waved the man away; but the old man stood firm and staring, bunched, chiseled, almost metallically tanned. The Indian wore a blue and white, large-checked shirt and faded levis. He had no shoes. Peterson saw black snakes unwind suddenly across the road, quickly from lily bed to lily bed. He rolled his window down and leaned out.

"How do I get out of here?" he called. "I need Route 6!"

The old Indian picked up a stone from the road. Peterson thought he was going to smash the windshield. The man walked slowly toward him. Peterson whipped his car into reverse. The engine stalled. The old Indian stood before him, kicking Peterson's license plate. The Indian strolled alongside the open window. He cleared his throat, threw his head way back. His long silvering hair billowed in the wind. He was squeezing the stone he'd picked up between his palms.

"Yes?" Peterson said.

The Indian touched the outside mirror.

"How do I get out of here?" Peterson asked.

The old Indian smiled at him. His teeth had grown over each other and were veined and unwashed like quartz. He rattled Peterson's car door.

"I need to get to Montana," Peterson said.

The old Indian laughed. He slapped the side of the car with his fist-sized stone.

"Hey!"

The old Indian shook Peterson's door again, harder. Then he pointed.

"I need to get to Montana! I just came here to see the light! Is that the way?"

The old man reached toward the sunglasses on the dashboard.

Peterson ground the ignition key. He backed away, showering the old man with dust. He caught an image of the man: stiff, diminishing. He reversed hard, found a turnaround, pressed on straight ahead, angry now, to get out. With each left he took, each right, each single and reverse switchback, he could hear his stones avalanching over each other in his trunk. He saw deer and beaver and fox, otter, groundhog, bittern, snowy egret. But not once did he catch sight of any asphalt or pavement. Then, an hour and a half or more later, he saw the same old man still rigid in the dust.

"What do I need to do to get *out*? Please! Tell me!"

The old Indian nodded. He touched the car. He touched himself. He pointed off down the road.

"O.K. — O.K.; sure." Peterson took an enormous chance. "Sure! Hop in."

The Indian moved stolidly to the passenger's side; he opened the door, entered. He smelled like tar to Peterson, tar and chalk. He instructed Peterson with his hands. They approached a house. The Indian started nodding. The house was one-story, hand-assembled of stone. The old Indian motioned Peterson to get out and walk with him toward it.

Peterson followed. They entered the doorless house. The interior was cool and mysterious. It tasted moist and like a cave. The stones that formed it, like those loose and clicking in Peterson's locked trunk, all carried emblems: a comb, a watchface, a phonograph spindle, an acoustical tile.

"What do you know about these stones?" Peterson asked. The Indian seemed preoccupied. "I . . . had a theory. But those high cliffs . . . I . . ." Suddenly Peterson couldn't catch his breath to speak. He pressed his hands against his thighs, kept them still. "How . . . ?" He felt static electricity in his hair, and a wind for which there was no source. Peterson found that his lips were chapped, bleeding; the blood tasted like salt. Before they'd capsized, Peterson had tossed the Jesuit a soda cracker. It had been too light. The wind had caught it and it had blown insane. "Not enough body!" the Jesuit had joked.

The old Indian squatted on the hard-packed floor and handed Peterson a cinnamon-colored fruit. It was irregular in shape, odd. Peterson wanted almost feverishly to ask more about the stones, but he couldn't. The fruit had spikes on it, infant thorns.

"Do I peel these off?" Peterson asked.

The old Indian rotated his hands together.

Peterson knelt and scraped away some of the spikes. He used his fingernails, then tasted the fruit. He incessantly formed questions inside himself about the imprints everywhere. The fruit seemed almost oversweet, tainted. It made Peterson retract his tongue. He lost his questions. *Should I . . . ? Might I . . . ? Is it possible that . . . ?* His eyes clouded. He felt his gums pucker, then the insides of his cheeks. *If I could just get out*, Peterson thought.

The old Indian rose and gestured Peterson up. He put both index fingers together, turned his body west, fingers together still. He held his arms horizontal and rigid, then raised them to an angle of about forty-five degrees. He repeated this three times.

"Out?" Peterson finally asked.

The old Indian nodded.

"You will show me the way out?" Peterson was shaking. His mind formed the single, curious word inside: *monastic.*

The old Indian nodded again. He motioned Peterson to follow. They approached a stone archway in the opposite wall of the house, draped over entirely with layerings of animal skins. The old Indian drew the curtaining aside. A girl sat alone inside on pelts. Her eyes glinted like bloodstone. She rose.

No more than twenty, Peterson thought: *His granddaughter.* The old Indian backed away quickly to the outer room. Peterson felt the calcium moistness of the stones. He tasted lime. His bones felt cold. The girl's eyes were fixed on him. He stayed his breath. The fossils were watching too. He observed the dark legs, thighs, hair, stomach, breasts, throat before him. He observed her skin. It was patterned lightly with clear glyphsigns: a cufflink, an amphetamine capsule, teeth of a zipper, a small cathode tube. The young Indian girl held her hand out.

Peterson backed away. "What do you want?" he asked. He heard his words echo: repeat, muffle, multiply as if he were inside a cave. "What do you want?" The girl sat still, her hand reaching without assault. She was beautiful, undeniably: dark, soft. Her skin had woodscent to it. The markings on her skin did not obscure her natural light, her very quiet ignition in the damp mineral dark. "What do you want?" Peterson whispered. Enormous lizards fed on vegetation in the North American swamps just outside. "What do you want?" He spoke the words to other women; other men; the ghost of the Jesuit; himself.

Peterson broke out through the animal skins. His eyes contracted in the light of the open room. "What do you want?" he shouted. "What do you want from me? Do you want me to take her? Do you want me to take her with me? I have to go. I need to go. It's important that I get to where I'm going. Montana! Arrive. On time. If that's the deal — if that's the only way out: then, O.K.! O.K., O.K., I'll take her!" Peterson was screaming. The old Indian smiled.

From the four corners of the room he gathered treasures, brought them to Peterson, set them down. There were animal teeth, animal eyes, viscera preserved in some light blue fluid in a mason jar. There were the skulls of hawks, the pelvis of a huge grizzly bear, a tanned hide pasted and spread with bright geometric moth and bufferfly wings. There were bunches of feathers, hanks of wildflowers, clusters of dried fruit, stalks of mint, any number of gnarled, quite unnameable tubers; a pouch of delicately dyed porcupine quills; rough, unpolished coral and topaz; green stones, blue stone, blood- and sun-colored stones. There were medicines and teas and body oils.

Peterson stood, accepting. He could not master the trembling in his bones. He did not know what the girl might be preparing in the next room. At last the old Indian presented — laying them one by one in a semicircle around Peterson on the hard earth floor — hand-carved, hand-painted wooden masks. The masks terrified Peterson; they were stark, unyielding, hard. The lips were bone-straight and sealed. The cheeks were clenched. The brows had an implacable look of impenetrable skull. The eyes were agate and without depth. Peterson had no thought of being, in any way, ungrateful; still he waved the brutish masks away. And the old Indian gladly rehung them around the walls of his small rockwork hut. Their sculpted faces were obscured, turned in against the stone, the features lost.

Peterson carried all the gifts out to his car and packed them in his trunk while the old Indian, on another lightly tanned piece of hide, drew him a map. The Indian used something like oil paint which he mixed himself in the cavity of a lens-shaped stone five or six inches across. The Indian moved his finger almost magically to paint each line. It was as if he were creating egress as he drew. Peterson stopped a moment and watched. He stopped his shaking. He could imagine ruts and rain-hollows occurring right under the old Indian's touch. He could imagine cicadas exploding left and right and getting out of the way. He could smell the sea, taste the noon weight of sun on kelp.

When nothing more remained to be carried out and the old Indian's chart lay complete, they went back into the house. The young girl appeared from the interior room. She was even more striking in light. Her lips were moist. Her hair moved like secret black flame. Her eyes caught a green and infinite space. Her bones connected like notes. She smiled at Peterson. He smiled back. She wore a single piece of print material, cinched at the waist with rawhide. She was barefoot.

"Where is where on this?" Peterson asked the Indian, indicating the map.

The old Indian pointed to a single dot placed on the leather surface in black, then pointed to his own earthen floor.

"Here," Peterson verified.

The old Indian nodded. Peterson felt relieved. He felt that, having established a base, he could find his way. He saw the old

man and young girl staring quietly at each other. He gave them
privacy and walked outside to wait. Waxwings were moving in low
shrubs, feeding on wild wineberry. Peterson watched a huge oval-
backed painted turtle. He stared off at the high granite cliffs; he
could no longer make out any emblems. He put his hands over his
eyes and felt his fingers vibrating. He wondered precisely what
departure sacrament was taking place inside the room. Did the two
have language? He had not heard any. Peterson caught the sound
of splashing but could not locate water.

At last the girl appeared. She came by herself and carried a
moderately large leather pouch. Peterson imagined it filled with
combs and hairbrushes. The girl shone; she did not reflect. It was
as if she took in all sunlight, condensed it, then gave it back. The
glyphs on her skin were her only shadows. Peterson opened the
car door. He imagined the old Indian absolutely motionless,
centered, in the room. The girl got in. Peterson crossed to his side
and entered. He set the key in the ignition. He spread the map on
the seat. The Indian girl watched. She did not seem sad, or distant, or at all afraid. It was an unusual thing for Peterson to do,
but he touched her. He turned the engine on. They started.

It took them hours to get out, into dark. At one place the road
was flooded. Peterson hauled dead fallen trees, it seemed endlessly,
from the dense, overcrowded woods; laid them down to build up
sufficient roadbed. His hands bristled with splinters. At another
point an enormous boulder blocked their way. The rock had can
opener prints covering it, placed almost as regularly as print. Peterson used his tire jack, some rusting fence wire he found in the long
grass, and another series of poles and felled trees to construct a
remarkable leverage apparatus and removed the stone. The girl
helped tremendously. When the rock finally rolled aside, Peterson
gave way, falling against the hood of the car. His lungs and breathing seemed coarse and pebbled. His shoulders felt wrung. At still
another point, around dusk, they took a turn and found themselves
totally surrounded by brush fire. Peterson experienced panic. He
thought his engine would explode. He sat, screaming at the flames:

"Bastards! I was coming through!" He took a large tire pump from his trunk, emptied six cans of beer into it, set the automatic transmission at LO, showed the Indian girl how to press gently on the accelerator, walked in front of the crawling car, screaming: *"Back! Back!"* — words almost magic — spraying the fire with hissing, pressurized beer. *"Floor it!"* he yelled finally, as he swept his arm in an appropriate gesture, jumped fast to the side, and saw her clear the last flames. Peterson ran and caught up. There was straight road ahead now.

When they finally saw Route 6, Peterson rocked and heaved. He shook. He stopped the car. Choking and vomiting, he kept tasting salt water in his lungs, kept feeling his ribs. The Indian girl moved close, held him, smoothed his skin. Peterson cried. He felt her fingers webbed on his stomach. "You have no idea . . . you have no idea, do you, why I'm . . . ?" But she only smiled at him, then lay her face and hair quietly on his arm. Peterson stopped crying; he laughed. He cried again. He coughed; he tried to stifle his coughing in his hands; his breath smelled like the silt from the lake bed. Tiny globes of rainwater shone from lupine beside the road. Rabbit fed quietly in the grass. He was *there*; Peterson finally managed to smile. He was *out*.

He almost slept but reconsidered. It was dark. The Indian girl stayed against him. Peterson shook his head. *Such things didn't just* . . . He felt knit with scar tissue. He moved to let the Indian girl out. He would show her how to hitchhike; someone would pick her up; she was bright; she'd learn words; it would be . . . Peterson's seatbelt caught him, the lock snagged. He became aware of his stiff hands, the nails cracked like mica. He imagined the Indian girl as a topless cocktail waitress in a bar in Oakland. He started up the car.

They drove west, stopping nights. The first night, in Blind River, Ontario, Peterson watched the Indian girl unwrap eighteen bars of motel soap, arrange and rearrange them on the counter top.

He watched her watch herself for more than an hour in the large frameless mirror. She would lift her hand, drop it, lift it again; tilt her head to one side, return it; smile, scowl, touch her nipples. She tried to find herself on the colored television. Peterson mixed them drinks, vodka and tonic. The Indian girl stacked the eyeleted ice cubes on her fingers and watched them melt. They slept together that night; she huddled close to him, clutching his elbow as if it were some stuffed, smiling toy. They were tired and sleep came quickly.

In the car she liked all the windows open, the radio on. She would lean her head way back against the headrest, smile, let the sunlight strike her, hum quietly. They bought food at markets and had picnics. The girl knew how to open plums with her fingernails. She loved wine. She had Peterson pour it into her cupped hands; then she drank. They found lakes, took their clothes off, swam. One time she vanished, diving, and Peterson felt a brutal visceral gap. They chased each other in and out of trees. Once they took whole fistfuls of lambert cherries and squeezed them inside up-stretched hands, feeling the juice run down their arms, licking it, throwing the pulpy pits at each other in satiric war, spreading the still sticky juice over one another's backs. Each taught the other. Peterson taught the girl language, words: "pool" and "vodka," "cross," "sun," "lumbago," "steel." "Africa." "Television." "Deep." "Raw-hide." "Sandlewood." "Mississippi." "Lungs." "Karma." "Overcome." "Panda bear." "Largo." "*Key* Largo." "Drowned." "Raspberry." "Tuna salad." "Fuse." "Future." "Coliseum." "Anthropomorphic." "Cock." What the girl taught Peterson was a kind of weightlessness, an ease. They spent nights together in Ironwood, Michigan; Detroit Lakes, Minnesota; Jamestown, North Dakota. They swam. Peterson bought clothes. They rubbed each other down with mineral oil in the sun. She began to call herself Lona. That began in Ironwood. They were eating peppermint ice cream with their fingers in the Royal Coach-man Motel, and the girl pointed to herself and said, "Lo-na."

"Lo-na," Peterson repeated.

And she'd nodded: "Lo-na."

Peterson told her about the Jesuit: his fierce intelligence, his Boston humor, his laugh. The girl's markings became gradually fainter. On the third morning, when they showered together in Detroit Lakes, Peterson noticed that the images were completely gone. He started choking on shower water. He saw a wilderness in his mind: swamp, rock outcroppings, giant vines. Then all he could see was the aluminum showerhead. Lona struck him on the back. His breathing regularized. He recognized fish patterns on the shower tiles. He dried himself and got dressed. He combed Lona's extraordinary hair for her while she watched green animated bears on the television. Peterson loved her laughter. He fed her half a nectarine. When he brought their bags out to the car he checked the stones still in the trunk. They were almost all unfossilized: smooth, round, and water-polished. Only the fern and fish's spine remained.

That same night, in Jamestown, Peterson decided to let Lona go.

The low North Dakota sun gave a bruised light to the still and cloud-traced western sky. They were at a place called Smith's Junction Diner. They had finished dessert and Peterson was smoking. Lona was standing with a group about her own age around a pinball machine. She had moved in close to watch. There were bells ringing and lights cool and bleating. One of the young men was talking. Lona's face shone in the colored bulbs. She was laughing and moving her body in a sort of dance, a motion half to the rhythm of the pinball, half to the juke box. She was eating Lifesavers. Helen Reddy was singing "Delta Dawn," music Lona had already learned from the car radio, and she sang along. There were muted undersounds of cups and silverware being washed, of the cigarette machine. Outside, Peterson heard a quick release of air brakes. His eyes closed. She was exceptional, he thought. How she surfaced! How she learned! He would only anchor her. She was dancing with a boy now, and even the waitress looked greedily on. They were both laughing. Peterson took two hundred dollars from his wallet, slipped it into Lona's large leather bag and, quietly, painfully, left.

He drove west, then north. Then turned around and drove east. He circled Jamestown through three changes in the height and color of its sky. At last he parked himself outside a dark and shut-down Chevron station, ringed by faint fishlike and petroleum smells. Insects crawled his windshield, skittered over their own kind stained there, dead. There was a dull taste, too, of humus. Peterson reached a hand behind him and touched his spine. It felt ancient, like some tooth or tool, gem or pottery chip, like some artifact. *We are our own archeology*, Peterson thought and felt profoundly unearthed.

He drove back to Jamestown. Lona stood, face pressed to the glass, like an emblem, beneath the on-and-off Smith's Junction Diner sign. She saw Peterson. He jumped out. She ran toward him. The diner sign stayed on.

Within a year, they claimed Montana and stayed. Lona stopped calling herself *Lona* and took on another name: *Rosa Swann*. Peterson mined. He learned to carve pine waterbirds. He began to whistle and sing. He even spread the rumor, out among the natives, that he was what he called a reformed Franciscan. No one knew what it meant. But they liked Peterson.

In time, Peterson and Rosa Swann established what became the most extraordinary Wild West show in the world. Horses danced. Bulls braved fire. Lariats made hoops and spirals in the air. Their arena sang.

And, everywhere, saddles glowed like primitive, sculptured stone.

The Phantom Mercury of Nevada

This is not science fiction. This is real! I swear. Real as light spreading over the desert, real as thunder in the Tuscaroras. Real as friendship: me and Ross and LaVelle. Real as any Mercury that ever grew to being in Detroit, its ignition firing, its spoked wheels making a blur; its radio blaring an all-night station miles away. Real as losing a nickel in a slot machine, or a dog under the wheels of a backing Bronco. *Real* — and such a mystery!

Still, I vowed I would keep it to myself. And I made LaVelle swear. I said: "LaVelle — whatever happens; if you and I get married or don't get married; if you decide to go off to Winne-mucca and sing with that group at the Star; or if you go with Mr. Forbes to Dallas — whatever. Please! Don't tell!" I had taken her on my trail bike up Mount Lewis and we had spent the night there, "engaged." The sun, blood-red, was just climbing in the east, beyond Dunphy, and reaching toward our own streets in Battle Mountain. I took a bluish-veined rock and nearly crushed my left pinkie finger to impress upon LaVelle that I meant what I said. *It was real! Ross Haine was missing.* That was all we knew or should ever say. He'd gone *off*. Maybe he'd gone to be a busboy, down at Stockman's in Elko like he sometimes said he would. But we should never breathe a word about what we felt had happened to Ross with the Phantom Mercury. Who knew? And LaVelle cried. And she sucked away the blood from my struck pinkie. And she said, "Yes, Jason! I promise! Yes!" But now LaVelle's gone. And my dreams are just about exploding. So . . .

My parents own the Owl Motel on Front Street. I live in unit 23; my younger brother, Richie, lives in unit 17; and my parents room behind the office. We're never full, but the motel, I guess, makes money; I've never heard anyone complain. I clerk seven to midnight, Mondays, Wednesdays, and Fridays; Richie, Tuesdays and Thursdays. And when my Grandfather Tombes comes up to visit from Arizona, *he* always clerks. We chip in. It really used to be fun. I could watch the Zenith or have Ross Haine over and we could both watch the Zenith. And checking people in, that was interesting. One time a man had driven all the way without stopping from Guatemala, South America. "Is this *the* Battle Mountain?" he asked; "Battle Mountain turquoise?" And I told him: Yes, it was; and he just lit up. And then I told him that I cut stones myself, that I had some really nice green and brown spider-webbed pieces and a brand new diamond micro drill and a MT-4S compact tumbler; and we talked rocks. He was a dark man. But now, of course, my shift is terrible. All the stuff on the Zenith is about Death. And Ross is gone. And now LaVelle. And so about all there is to do is sit there, scared really, wondering if the Phontom Mercury is going to come down again out of the Tuscarora Mountains.

I never want to drive. It sounds funny to say that, because I always wanted to. I mean, I'd be going to bed in my unit at maybe one A.M., and a guest would pull his Pontiac or Chevy in and the lights would burn through my curtains, and I'd think, "God! Three more years!" Then: Two more! Then: A year and a half! Then: November! And I'd actually *dream* about this one particular Torino, three lanes wide, with its high beams on, climbing through the Humboldts toward Sparks. But now — Jeez!

Some cattle went. That was first. A family named Pollito had a small range on the Dunphy side of Battle Mountain up Rock Creek. And they started missing head. Their son, Lyle, knew Richie and Richie told me.

"How many are gone?" I asked.

"Six."

The next day Richie said: Eight. And the next: Eleven. I talked to Ross Haines, and he and I took our bikes up to Pollitos' land. It was early September, dry, the north creek barely running. Everything seemed brittle. And there was a flinty smell in the air.

We parked. Ross had gotten a quart of beer and we opened that. We sat down by some yews. We knew something was going to happen. We didn't say anything to each other before, but we talked about it afterward — and we *knew*. We picked yewberries, rolled them around between our fingers and tossed them, and watched the sun fall somewhere beyond Reno.

"Would you ever shoot anyone?" Ross asked me.

The insects and the tree frogs had started up. I didn't say anything; I just threw about three yewberries into where it was dark.

"I hope I get to be in a war," Ross went on. He said it felt like he and I were on sentry duty. We'd both shot chukar and grouse. I wasn't sure what made him think of it.

But then . . . both of us leaned forward and looked up. Neither talked. There was something . . . I don't even know if I can describe it any better than that: something high and far away in the Tuscaroras. And it was coming down. And it was coming down . . . and it was coming down . . . and it was coming down. And we were both leaning forward straining for it. And whatever it was — we never knew what that night — *increased*; that was the word we could both agree on; it *increased*. And it increased enough so that at one point we weren't looking up and away any more; we were looking all around us. "Shit! I wish I'd brought my gun!" I heard Ross whisper. And then we found ourselves looking up again — because, whatever it was, it was going home, up, away, *decreasing* now, ridge to ridge, canyon to canyon.

The next day Richie told me that three more of the Pollitos' steers had gone, and I didn't say anything to him about our being up there. I just found Ross.

We tried to agree. We tried to write down some things that both of us could say we'd seen or felt, or that had happened. We made a list. *Rumbling* was on the list, slight rumbling; we thought a while about the word *vibration*, but *rumbling* won. I was near a slide once, a rock slide close to Tonopah, and it was like that. And there was a . . . we hit upon the word *fluorescent*: a *fluorescent* glow. It wasn't bright. We argued that it could have been just

kind of the after-sunset glow, but then we had to say that it wasn't;
it was whiter, greener, like the light in Mr. Iatammi's welding shop,
seen maybe a mile away. And there was a chemical smell, just
slight. All of these things were just slight; it took us nearly three
hours just to get the four of them down, to agree. But we'd both
coughed at least once. So Ross wrote *sulphur*. And the last item
was the weirdest of all. I mentioned it kind of as a joke, but then
Ross agreed and said that, right, his teeth had hurt him too —
when whatever-it-was was the closest. So that was it: a rumbling,
a fluorescent glow, sulphur, and our teeth hurt.

LaVelle and I were friends. It hadn't gotten physical yet,
except, I know, in my head. Some of the kids called her Frenchie—
LaVelle Barrett — which was kind of exciting anyway; but she had
a really nice singing voice and played O.K. on the guitar. We
joked. She kept asking when I was going to take her to my motel,
and I'd say something back and we'd laugh. But we also talked
about serious things. Her father had shot a man, and the man had
died, and so her father was serving out a term for it in the Wyoming
state prison. LaVelle opened up to me about it one day when we
were walking by the Reese River, and she cried, and I just held her
and let her, and I guess that was the main reason for our friendship.
Her mother was strict. She made LaVelle keep pretty exact hours.
Her mother dealt at the Owl Club Casino (no relationship to our
Owl Motel), but she always checked on her. Anyway, after Ross
and I experienced what we experienced that first night, I told
LaVelle.

"*Take* me!"

"Well..."

"I'd like to see!"

I spoke to Ross. He said sure; but let's, the three of us, keep
it at that. So we decided upon the following Thursday night.

We went up at just the same time. LaVelle had a horse named
Tar (she was supposed to just be out riding), and we met her at
a certain place, east on I-80; and then the three of us, on Tar —
poor Tar! It was crowded — rode on up.

It wasn't quite sundown, so we investigated. "What if Mr. Pollito sees us and shoots us?" LaVelle asked. I said: "I'll just tell him I'm Richie's brother and that we're trying to catch his rustlers. He'll be grateful." Then LaVelle found a rock with a long white-silver scrape mark along it.

"That's paint!" Ross said.

"No," I disagreed. "That's just bruised quartz crystals in the rock."

"The hell you say!" Ross, for some reason, got angry. "That's paint!"

At sunset we all gathered back at the same yew bushes. Ross pointed high to the north. "It'll start up there," he told LaVelle. LaVelle looked at me. She started stroking Tar's neck. She fed him a piece of sugar. Then it began, just like the time before — everything on our list, *everything*: rumbling, fluorescent glow, sulphur, our teeth hurt. Tar spooked. We thought he was going to run off for a minute. He shook his head. It must have hurt *his* teeth. LaVelle had taken my hand. It made me sweat a little. "Gol! What was that?" she asked.

The next day, Rich told me: "Another steer!"

We knew we were on to something. Ross, LaVelle, and I talked. We wanted to see whether we could add anything else to our list. "Did it trace a path?" I asked them, because I sort of had that in my mind.

"Yeah!" Ross said. His eyes just got *large*.

"Yes," LaVelle nodded.

"Coming down — and going up!" Ross moved his hand in a kind of oval.

So that was the fifth thing on our list: *an oval path*.

We tried to decide whether we should tell Mr. Pollito what we were up to, so that he wouldn't pick us off by accident; you know, shoot us. But LaVelle was concerned about her mother. So we agreed that we would just all try very hard to be careful. I went walking with LaVelle after our discussion that day, and we wandered into the woods and stood for a while and kissed. It was the very first time. I was very aware of birds there, for some reason, and I asked LaVelle later if she was. "Not particularly," she said.

Our next trip to Pollitos', we decided to locate a little more north and west. It was closer to the grazing areas, where the cattle were. LaVelle was worried about Tar. He had shied the last mile and a half at least; he had tried very much to get his own head and lead us totally someplace else. "Look at his flanks," LaVelle pointed. His flanks were jumping. "And his mane!" She said the hair was taller than usual there, stiffer. But I couldn't see it.

"Why don't we ride him back a ways?" I suggested. "Where he's more relaxed. Tie him. Then you and I can jog on back to here. We've got another half-hour or so — before dark."

So we did. We tied him and left him where he could reach a good amount of grass. I kissed LaVelle again. She was kind of against a tree, and she pressed herself, it seemed really hard, against me and I let one hand slip down from her shoulder, and she made a sound which I had never heard. But then we ran together, holding hands, back to where Ross was, anxious. "Hurry!" he said when he saw us.

That night everything happened — and *more*. To our list we added: *always just after sunset* (which we could have added after the second time), *heat* (we all agreed we'd felt a rise in heat), and — LaVelle was the one who pointed this out, but when she said it, both Ross and I had to go along — *music*; there was some kind of tinny or metal or something *music*. And that was the night of the first really great discovery: *tire tracks*. There were tire tracks in a meadow nearby where some steers still were. LaVelle suggested that they belonged to Mr. Pollito's pickup maybe, but working in a motel and being as interested in driving as I was, I knew they were not pickup tracks; they were *car* tracks. And they were fresh. And they were *real*. Again, I tell you this is not science fiction. Somehow a car had come down through that meadow. And not long ago! Also, Ross thought he saw something: "I saw something, I *know* it!" he said; "kind of a *car* or something like that shape!" But neither LaVelle or I could honestly go along with it, so we didn't write it down.

The next day, trying to be casual, I said: "Hey, Rich! How're Pollitos doing with their stock?"

"Weirdest thing!" he said to me. "Last night . . . !"

"Lose more?"

"No, but they found one this morning — *weird* — dead! Lyle said it looked as if it had been hit by a huge rock. Or a *car*."

Oh, and one more kind of connected thing happened before the *true* time, before the time when we actually stood there in the yellow-and-almost-black light, stood with no breath in us at all and actually *saw* the Phantom Mercury. A Mr. Forbes came into town from Dallas. He stayed at the Big Chief Motel and not the Owl, and so I hardly saw him. But his reason for coming to Battle Mountain was LaVelle. He found her and told her that he had promised her father — who he knew very well and respected — that he would do all that he could to bring her back with him from Battle Mountain to Dallas. He told her that there were quite a few what he called "peripheral circumstances" connected with her father's shooting and killing of the other man. And that he felt that it would really be "to her best advantage" (LaVelle's, that is) to get what she could get out of the house here and return there, to Dallas, with him. They talked for several days, and she would report it back to me. She told him that what she wanted, she thought, was to be a lead singer with a group; and he had told her that that was fine; that was a good ambition; and that he would do all that he could for her. At first she thought the whole thing was just ridiculous, but after a couple days, she began to look on it, kind of, as a dilemma.

Ross got a gun. It was a .45 pistol, made in Peru, he said, but he wouldn't tell us where he got it: "Guns are available." That was it! He nailed a Clorox jug to a stump near the Reese River and marked it up worse than a Keno card with shots. I asked him what he thought he would shoot at when whatever-it-was went by the next time. He said he didn't know.

Meanwhile, LaVelle and I got on. She asked me to listen to

her sing. She'd bring her guitar, and we'd climb Mt. Lewis, then
sit and she'd play "Leaving' on a Jet Plane" or "Killin' Me Softly,"
and I'd undo the back buttons on her blouse slowly and when she
finished, she'd lean forward so that the two halves of her blouse
would fall to either side and she'd just stare out toward Winne-
mucca and Reno, west, and say to me: "Jason? Do you think I'm
good enough?" And I'd say, "LaVelle, I don't know." But before
I could finish saying that, she'd ask another question, insert it:
"What do you think of Mr. Forbes?" And so I'd just have to tell
her again: "I don't know, LaVelle. I don't know what to tell you.
He seems short." And then I'd look at her, at her undone blouse
kind of riffling in the mountain wind. And at about that same time
she'd stand up and walk forward and press one cheek against an
aspen tree, and then reach in back of her and do her blouse up
again. She was making up her mind.

On the final night — I call it *the final night*, although that was
true only for Ross, and even then, not exactly true — we all told
our parents we were going back to the school auditorium after
supper to attend the annual Battle Mountain Gem Show. We lied.
We left early. Ross brought his gun. LaVelle was humming. We
rode Tar part way, but on the edge of Pollitos' property, left him,
tied, and hiked.

"I'm planning to stand right where the tire tracks were," Ross
told us. "How about you?"

We looked at him. He was carrying his gun. It was a warm
night. It felt like summer coming on, sort of, instead of fall. The
sky was that color green.

"Have you two gone together yet?" Ross asked us, out of
nowhere. LaVelle looked off. I shook my head. "Geez," he said,
"It's just a question!" And he pointed his gun off at an old, gray
junked refrigerator door. We heard our boots and LaVelle's clogs
especially, pressing down on rocks all along the bed.

When we got there, where the marks had been, we stood. It
was . . . I don't know. Except for insects and the diesel sound of a
semi down somewhere on I-80 below, it was quiet. Dark was close.

And there was the smell — I guess they'd been there earlier — of Pollitos' stock. It made me want to be beside LaVelle, to touch her, even her levis, which I tried but didn't manage too well.

We checked the air. We looked up as far as we could into the Tuscaroras. They seemed to change their shape. I'd heard a story once about a cougar who was supposed to live high up in them, one that nobody had been able, ever, to kill. His fur looked blue. And somebody had started the rumor — maybe it was an Indian; maybe it was a Shoshone story, anyway — that you could bring him down only with an arrowhead chipped out of black matrix Battle Mountain turquoise.

Ross stationed himself in the path. "I'm ready," he said. LaVelle and I stood on either side, a little away from the tracks. The Tuscaroras got dim. The sun set. The tree frogs started. I heard Ross checking the cylinder of his gun. I heard LaVelle and myself, across from each other, breathing.

"We're going to see it," I said. I don't know what, even, brought the words out.

"I know," LaVelle whispered.

"I saw it last time," Ross picked up the low, quiet tone of LaVelle. We were waiting.

Then things began. Way up. No sound, but a greenish-yellow flare, like heat lighting; the first time, not so bright; the second time, much brighter.

We were quiet.

Then the heat lightning or whatever it was flared again, this time down a ways, closer in. "I know," both Ross and I said together. Ross called out: "Touch the stones!" We saw him in the shadows reaching down and touching the stones in the creek bed. So we both reached down and touched the stones ourselves, and when we did, we could feel them shaking. "Gol!" LaVelle said. It was like the stones had little motors.

Then it flashed a fourth time. It was down now, coming down, increasing. And there was that chemical smell that we had all agreed on — but not just slight. I heard LaVelle say: "Jason!"

I said, "It's all right." But Ross didn't say anything. I touched my jaw. I could taste my fillings along with the chemical smell all along the top of my mouth and in my nose. Everything grew. I heard LaVelle making sounds, halfway between crying and the sounds she'd made the night I touched her against the tree. "Get down," I said. "Tar!" she called out. "Tar!" And then: "Jason!" Ross was keeping quiet. It got warmer. Then warmer still.

The glow was coming. LaVelle fell down. It was sort of that welding light. And I could barely stand up myself because of the shaking in the stones. There was an engine sound — and then another sound: like the sound of guitar music turned way up late at night, coming from far away, from some place like Maine or West Virginia on a car radio. *"It's a car!"* I called out. *"You bet it is!"* Ross called back. We could see the shape. The shape was coming down the creek bed, glowing, rumbling, giving off showered light, then crossing the meadow just above us. Ross started piling stones up in a dam. The shape went out of sight behind some trees. "Look out!" I called. He said, "Don't worry!" LaVelle was screaming. Then it broke through the trees where we were. "Get back!" I cried. LaVelle was screaming with every breath. "It's a Mercury!" I yelled to Ross. I recognized its grill. God, it was traveling! Then Ross's gun started, again and again, exploding! I smelled gunpowder and hot rubber and transmission oil all at once, and my own body, and, I swear, LaVelle's. I saw the Mercury go by us down the creek bed, and it was all silver and dented white, pitted all over like the moon. *God, it was real!* Ross's gun rang out, then stopped. The Mercury revved once, then entered some trees just below. *It was huge, man!* It was the hugest Mercury, I know, I've ever seen. It was more huge than a Lincoln, even, or a Pontiac!

It was dark. I was sweating. The radio music was in the air, moving, traveling always with the Phantom Mercury. LaVelle was stretched out, rocking, making a kind of sob. There was no moon visible. And I couldn't see Ross. "Ross! It's turned!" I called out. "Ross!" But he didn't answer. I saw the light, saw it turn its oval and start up, north, through a meadow, then begin to climb. "It's going back!" I shouted. LaVelle seemed in pain. I went to her. I knelt. She grabbed hold of me and held me; she was strong. She smelled like Tar. She tried to but couldn't form any words. I said, "That's all right," and I kissed her. She was full of sounds.

I turned my head to one side and called out "Ross!" again. But nothing came. Everything was fading. The light was flickering up into the Tuscaroras. I could see it. And it didn't look huge any more. It just looked like some backpackers with a Coleman lamp. And the stones were nearly still. And the air tasted burnt. That remained most, and the heat. My skin was dry in places, and wet in others. LaVelle calmed down. The first words she said to me, looking up, were, ". . . the music!" I didn't know what she meant; I didn't know what to say. I kissed her on the mouth again. We held it. Then I heard a stone turn, down from us, and I tried again: "Hey, Ross . . . ?"

Someone was standing in the dark. I helped LaVelle and we walked along the dry and now-empty creek bed where the Mercury had come. And Ross was there. He was standing in it, staring up through the night.

"Hi," I said. I squeezed LaVelle. I wanted her to feel that I was there.

Ross nodded.

"You O.K.?" I asked.

He was quiet. He picked up a stone and threw it. It was a white stone and I could see it leaving his hand for just a second or two. But then it went out, like a candle. And we heard it land maybe a hundred feet away. "I shot the driver," Ross told us.

"Are you serious?" LaVelle asked.

"I shot him." He was straight-faced. "That driver's got to be dead." He picked up another stone and threw it; this one was dark.

We hiked to Tar. We didn't talk. He seemed happy to see us. We mounted him and rode him down back into town. It was maybe nine o'clock.

What happened next was chance. We hadn't planned it, but none of us really wanted to go on along to our places and go to bed, so we decided to go to the Cascade Bowling Alleys and Roller Skating Rink and skate a bit. So we did. LaVelle took Tar home. She said her mother probably would be mad, but that it didn't matter. Ross and I understood.

Inside the Cascade it was pretty wonderful, in fact. It's nice to go around in what's not really dark, but not really light either, with one of those mirror-balls in the middle tossing off spots of colored light. It's nice to skate. It's nice just to have records on, too, and to be going around, just be going around and around and around *together*, with your girl in the middle and your very best friend from all your years in school on the other side. And to not be touching the ground! Do you know what I mean? Do you know what I'm talking about? I mean, to be circling and floating there in the Cascade Bowling Alleys and Roller Skating Rink with just *ball bearings* under your toes and heels, is *nice*.

We went outside after ten and just stood together. I'll always remember our feet on the ground again in the dark. It had gotten cool. Ross was quietest. We said: *See you in school tomorrow*, all of us. I remember. *See you in school*; each one; and then, each one: *Yeah . . . Yeah . . . Right . . . See you*. Then Ross turned away. And we watched him. His levi jacket looked like it had been chipped from stone. I hugged LaVelle, sort of. *Why weren't we talking? Any of us? Why?* And then I walked her home. The next day Ross wasn't in school or anywhere. Then, four months later . . . LaVelle.

I know the Mercury got them. Ross especially. I see that heat lightning high in the Tuscaroras now at dusk, and I think: *Maybe he's driving it!* That could be. *Maybe he's the driver now.* And if I go up to Pollitos' meadow at the end of some afternoon and wait — for the rumbling to start and the welding light and for my teeth to hurt — then Ross will come! And LaVelle! And we can all drive the Phantom Mercury down to the Cascade and skate. And Ross will be wearing his chiseled levi jacket. And LaVelle's voice and guitar will be in the air. And I can touch LaVelle again. And taste her. And be Ross's friend. It would be better than seeing Mr. Forbes eating broasted chicken in the Miner's Room at the Owl Club all by himself. Or waking up at headlights.

In fact, I'm sorry that I was ever curious, actually. About the world and about the real things that are in it. I mean . . . why do people disappear?